BONES

by

Chenjerai Hove

❖

Illustrated by Luke Toronga

❖

BAOBAB BOOKS
HARARE

First published in 1988 by Baobab Books
(a division of Academic Books (Pvt.) Ltd.
P.O. Box 567, Harare, Zimbabwe)

This second edition (reset) published in 1990

Reprinted 1999

© Chenjerai Hove

© Illustrations Luke Toronga

Cover design: Maviyane Pike

Printed and bound in Harare, Zimbabwe, by
Mazongororo Paper Converters (Pvt.) Ltd.

ISBN 0-908311-03-6

Chenjerai Hove was born in Mazvihwa, Zimbabwe. Writer, editor and poet, his published works include **Poems Inspired by the Struggle for Zimbabwe, Up in Arms** and **Red Hills of Home.** The latter two received special commendation by the judges of the Noma Award. His first novel in English, **Bones** won for Chenjerai Hove and Baobab Books the Zimbabwe Book Publishers' Association 1988–89 First Prize for Literature, and in 1989, the prestigious Noma Award for Publishing in Africa. **Bones** has been translated and published in many languages including Danish, Dutch, German, Japanese, Norwegian and Swedish; as well as being published in English in the Heinemann African Writers Series.

For the women whose children did not return
sons and daughters
those who gave their bones
to the making of a new conscience,
a conscience of bones, blood
and footsteps
dreaming of coming home some day
in vain.

1 **Janifa**

SHE asked me to read the letter for her again today, Marita, every day she comes to me, all pleading, 'Janifa, read the letter again for me, please read it, read it all the time for me if you have the strength,' but I just read it, for the first few days, like those little letters girls receive from naughty boys . . . I love you, you are my margarine, my butter, my peanut butter for my heart . . . But she calls me to read the letter all the time without end, even in the night, everybody else asleep in their huts, on their mats, but she still wants to hear what he wrote to me. Marita, I say all the time, you shame me, I feel ashamed when I read this letter, a love letter to me. But for you I will read it, for you and nothing else, but the shame in my heart weighs on me like a stone. Can you think of anything that can shame a young girl more than a letter from the boy? But Marita still calls it the best thing I have ever done for her. To bring that letter to her, just to say to her, Marita, he once wrote me a letter which I still keep with me. Yes, in truth, he wrote me a letter which I will be too ashamed to read to you. I do not know how it is with me, when I read it I smile as if it were the best thing that ever happened to me, just like that. I smile as if to say I would have loved him if he was still here. Strange, strange really how such small things take us this far. But Marita stares at me, gaping, while the soot from the burning leaves and grass gathers in her mouth as she stares at me . . . speechless, without a word from her mouth, just her heart telling me that I have something which is more important than I know. The first day she came to me, walking in the sun, sweating on the forehead, to say she wanted a few words with me: Yes, what is it, mother? I say. She stares at her feet, feet cracked with neglect, and lifts up her coarse finger to point at the nearby ant-hill. Can we go out, behind the ant-hill so that

7

we can be ourselves there? she says without any sign of anger in her voice. 'Come behind the ant-hill so that no one can steal with their ears,' she says, removing a few pieces of dry meat stuck in her teeth. Then I feel old, like the old women when they have a few words to share about the mischief of their husbands.

I remember one day when two women came to share the secrets of their husbands behind the ant-hill where I was helping myself. They were so full of stories in their hearts they could not wait to see if there was anybody behind the bushes. I just sat there long after I had finished what I went to do. How could I stand up in the middle of their secret? So I just sat there, behind their backs, with the smelly thing under my buttocks. Yes, the men are strange, very strange. They are like children. How could Mungai's husband be caught with such a slim, ugly woman despised by everybody in the village? As for me, if I am caught with another man, it must be a real man whose thing satisfies me. But Mungai's husband is something else . . . You never know, mother of my mother, that woman might have something to her more than we see. Can't you see he is even more determined to keep with her than before?

He really wants to keep her like a mother baboon keeping its little one. They are now like pot and fireplace, always together like a tree and a leaf. Do you know that some women know how to please husbands more than anything else? Never mind their bad cooking and all that, but when night comes, they know the language of the night. They make a man swear by his ancestors never to leave her. Maybe she is like that, hot blood and other things . . .

When they left, I had learnt that a woman is not simply her good looks. It was so quick. Like lightning. Just coming from the shivering lips of the women themselves, dangling their breasts right there in front of me sitting behind a bush. Even the smell of what I was doing did not seem to bother them. They knew where they were so they wouldn't bother at all. Do it in

8

the hut and they scream about the smell of these things, they send you away like a devil, not the child that came out of their own stomach.

'Tell me about this letter, is it in his own hand, written by him?' she says to me, froth coming out of her mouth, her blood hot.

'Yes, but why do you ask? He wrote it to me at the school and the teacher called me names when he found it in my other book.' . . . You bitch, all you keep in your dirty mind is love letters, nothing else. Take this rubbish and throw it in the rubbish pit, you prostitute of prostitutes . . . But I could not throw it away, my blood refused. So I took it outside, hid it in a place only my breast knew. I took it when we left school, and ran home, feeling that I had won something which the teacher couldn't give to me. That was the first letter a boy ever wrote to me, with his own hands, sitting somewhere, hiding from his parents to write a letter to me. I felt my blood do all sorts of things, then saw how I should hide it even from him so that he continued to think that I had thrown it in the lavatory as the teacher had commanded. They command, you know. They command even my own parents to send this or that, or else your son, your daughter, will be out of school for ever. They command. So I told him one day that I had thrown the letter in the lavatory, right in the smelly mess of all the stomach troubles of the whole school. From that day he did not speak with me . . . I will kill you, I will cut your head off for you. You bitch, bitching around with the teacher when you should choose people of your age. From that day, he injured my heart in all sorts of ways, as if I had swallowed all the needles on this farm, all of them, pains from even the tip of my breasts. Even when I failed at school, I felt I had also failed with him, failed him too. Failing all of us in one word like that. I don't know how the heart gets injured, but mine was cut into pieces that day when he said that. He said it over and over again in my dreams, in my food, in my clothes, and I felt death come over me like a flood. Then I felt I should tell you about it, the letter, I have a letter from him, his own words, and I felt a load of fire had been removed from my heart. Yes, I have the letter

9

even though I know that I would never marry him. How can I marry a terrorist, do they not say a terrorist eats people without roasting them? Do they not say a terrorist takes the wives of other men, sleeps with them before the eyes of their very husbands, then asks the parents to roast their children for him? I cannot marry a terrorist, a killer who kills his own mother.

'But he is my son,' she says, gentle tears dripping from her eyes. 'I did not teach him to eat people. I did not teach him to sleep with every woman he met on the way to the water well. I did not teach him to lead the life of a dog. I also taught him to respect the truth, to laugh only with those who liked the truth,' she says. 'Can you be kind enough to read for me the letter he left, it is the only thing that can tell me a little about him? Be kind, be kind to those who do not know how to skin a goat. Skin it for them so that they can say you saved them from the mouth of death. You are a well brought-up girl, a girl my boy knew could cook for him without putting poison in the food. A girl who would kneel for him while he talked with other men as if he was not seeing the woman who made him leave his own parents. Be good to me, the woman who would have been happy to be your mother-in-law. The mother of your husband, the one you would kneel for as I did to his own father. A sister to me because I knelt to his own father the same way you would kneel to him. Can you still continue to carry a hard heart when mine has melted into all this begging?' . . . I feel my heart melting, tears swelling in my eyes, and I say to her . . . 'Mother, wait, I will fetch the letter now and read it for you. It is our letter, you bore the son that wrote this letter, and he would have left you to live with me till his head grew white hairs. I will take you to a secret place where I can read the letter to you all by ourselves. Do not beg me like that, do not make me feel so big, giving me so much respect that it can kill me with pride in the whole farm . . .' So I run to my mother's hut, the one from which the smoke is already telling of the small pot sitting on it. The flies in there have not taken the letter away. I know nobody would take it away, even my own mother

10

stops my father from using any papers in there for rolling his own cigarettes . . . no, do not use that piece of paper, it's for the girl, the schoolgirl, child of school. Remember the other day you rolled your tobacco in her school report. You want to do it again so that teachers can laugh at us because of our ignorance? People do not laugh at ignorance, but they only laugh at its owner if he goes around parading it on the whole farm. How do you know what is written on it when you do not know how to write even your own name? Leave the child's papers alone. She is not the one who did not send you to school. Do you not boast about how you used to wrestle with teachers who tried to stop you from running away from school? Leave the child's things alone . . . she says as she pushes his hand away from the letter which I have always kept in the same bag, the *nhava* which his own brother made for me because he says I am the one who will give him cattle for the bride-wealth to bring home his fifth wife.

I run back into her hands like a child, like a child who has been sent by the other children to go and steal some maize cobs to bring to them so that they can chase away hunger in the forest where they are herding cattle. I run into her with all my body sweating like a spring, pouring out painful sweat and hot breath. She smiles at me and takes me by the hand like her own child . . . 'You have removed the things which were in my heart,' she says, searching with her eyes for a place to sit so that she can hear the words of her long-gone son from my lips.

'It is good to send children to school,' she says as she stretches her eyes from bush to bush, making sure that all those who might be relieving themselves there know that she can see them. 'It is good to send children to school, my child. Children should not be kept at home like cats and dogs,' she says, scratching the back of her head as if something has bitten her. She does not want to complain about these little biting things. She knows that the pain of the little bitings does not kill. 'It is this pain of my son which kills,' she says to me.

I start reading it, putting the boy's voice into the words so that

11

she can remember how he used to speak. I read and read without looking at her, but what's this breath that is moving the little bit of grass near my mouth? She is already leaning against me, listening, her eyes glowing and her breath bursting like a harsh wind. She is listening and telling me all about the boy who was good at school although I know the teacher used to say the best he could be was a thief because for that he would not need any course; that he would spend half his lifetime in jails, with high fences and walls where you need a mountain for a ladder to come out. They lock you in there and melt the keys so that you receive all your little bits of food from a small hole, the teacher would say. As for those who like women, like this boy, the teacher would say, not smiling, they put you behind the walls and fences and then show you naked women through a small hole so that you suffer. If you don't read your books, then the choice is jail, he would say, smoking his cigarette with the contented heart of one who is enjoying the work of his own hands, something he has made himself with his own sweating hands. Life is hard vafana, he would growl with the satisfaction of eating what everybody else thirsted for but would not have . . .

'He was such a boy, this one,' she says pointing at the letter. My mother will eat from the pot of your own hearth, and we will have children, not like the children of the farm foreman, but the teacher Mandindi's, with small bicycles to pedal . . . 'That is him, my son,' she says. 'The one who would have made me a grandmother, a good grandmother with children to run around playing with the mud, you, their mother, running after them to remove the mucus on their noses, my own son of this stomach which you see here without much food. His grandfather was like that, always dreaming of hunting trips and spears, sharp spears which he knew how to throw. You see, he was such a man, his grandfather, a quiet man who spoke with his whole heart. Of course, he took large amounts of snuff, sniffing, his moustache dancing all the time, dancing feverishly like a little forest shaken by the wind.'

'But why am I telling you about his grandfather? Why, why

12

waste your ears with all these things which an ear should not bother to remember, ears have better things to store than this. Better things useful for life. You are only a child with small breasts trying to come out like the small horns of a small bull. The world is still large for you, too many unspoken words, too many unheard voices, so no need for me to fill your head with rags of stories. After all, you have your own dreams to carry you along, dreams of young men and children to walk with you the path of life, not old women like me crying about a lost son, maybe one dead but with no grave to console her. No, I need not do that to you, you, the intestines of another woman of my own age. No, not to spill my own wounds into the heart of a young girl who needs to breed the plants of her own life for herself and for her people. No. Not at all. That must not happen.'

'Young girl, reader of my child's only letter to you, my eyes have seen what you have not seen. Many wounds have healed on this chest of mine. Many wounds. Many scars. Most of us women are one big scar, a scar as big as the Chenhoro dam from which farmer Manyepo waters his crops, vast, never drying. I will say this to you, I am one big wound, my child. One big wound without medicines or herbs. You know, they say the medicine for burdens of the heart is talk, but I have talked and talked, and I seem to talk more and more without cure. I once was a girl like you, erect breasts, full of dreams of my people, full of the stories of my people in my heart, craving to nurse my own child, my own seed so that my people will not say that I let them down. I broke the water-pot which my ancestors asked me to bring home. No. But what did I do? I burned to share my nights with a man, that man who would feel he had a queen in me. The one who would drive a whole herd of cattle to my father to say . . . Here is the bride-wealth, you gave me a bride for whom I am prepared to empty the cattle pen of my father in order to have her come to live with me . . .'

'But what happened? When everything had been done, I went to live with him, and for many years, the seed did not come.

The man planted his seed in me, but the soil inside me could not make it grow to a plant. Haunting and being haunted. Bad dreams, bad words, bad food, everything took on the colour of blood. And I thought I would cry for ever inside me. Right inside the inside of my heart. Then names came . . . you witch, you day-witch, you who ate the roots of your own womb, devourer of herbs which no herbalist can reverse . . . and the wounds of my heart burnt me till I was as thin as grass.'

'You see, my husband does not even talk about that child. Four years now, he has gone . . .' and the woman lifts a parade of four fingers in the air in a manner that makes me think they are withered, stiff like sticks on a dry branch of the *mupani* tree. 'Four years but he does not mention the name of the boy unless beer has loosened the knots of his mind. Then he pours out all the dirt he can allow to pass through his mouth without vomiting. Dirty words, dirty curses, dirty deeds of things that cannot be mentioned to live ears. But I shut my mouth and only look as if all that dirt were medicine that I should take for a bad disease. Just imagine, bitter medicine that I should take to cure the illness of my insides, the illness of my womb which refused to take his seed. Just imagine him shivering with fits of anger against me, spitting into the fire as if I have passed bad air, imagine. A hard life, this. A very hard life for a woman left alone on this farm. If my own father were alive I would have gone back to him to ask for his medicine in order to cure his own daughter who has fallen prey to barrenness. But no, I go on listening to the torture of my ears, the torture of my heart by those who have words as sharp as a razor. Words that eat into one like a bad disease which eats even into the bones of the victim . . .' she says as she makes the skin of her face wrinkle in my eyes to show me that she still can move the folds of her work-hardened skin, alive. Alive, breathing the soot of Manyepo's harvests. Walking to the river to bathe in the hot sun possessed here by Manyepo. She sighs her burdens off like one who has known them for too long. One who lives for these burdens which tire the soul. The soul. Marita, she kneels on

14

the brown soil with her cracked knees, and then caresses the few leaves that she tears away from their mothers.

The cloth on her head is torn and soiled with mud. She has carried the water-pot from the well for a long time. The cloth helps her head not to crack. There are other things she still has to carry. Things she does not know because they are things of the heart. She will carry them silently as she has done before, resolute. She feels the pain sink its jaws into her all the time. But she seems to take it all in one blow without telling too many people. Her lips are too busy containing the pain to go shouting behind the hills and streams of the farm. Nobody will listen. Nobody is used to listening to her. She says one word and stares at me. Maybe she thinks I cannot breathe any more. She shakes her head, with her mouth wide open, and then spits on the moist dust. The rains have come, but they do not seem to spit enough. She will help them spit on Manyepo's soil. Yes, this is Manyepo's soil. Marita will be here all the time. She is part of Manyepo's soil. She works it. She eats it. She breathes it. She feels it in her insides.

'Marita, your heart is full of your son. It is full of nothing else except your son,' I say.

'What else can I fill it with? What else can I put into it?'

'I do not know,' I mumble. 'But you are strong, very strong . . .'

'If I were strong, then I would fill my heart with something else.' She winces before her face becomes a shadow to me. She seems to be talking with the soil, the grains of sand behind this ant-hill.

2 **Janifa**

NOW that the woman is dead, my heart swells. Marita, why did you insist on going alone? Don't they say a journey is two people? You know I would have come with you, if only you had whispered into my ears. I would have run away with you to the city where they say it's daylight from start to finish. Who knows, I would have helped you carry all those burdens of the heart which weighed so heavily on you. Burdens that ate into you like a sickness. Marita, the city is like the throat of a crocodile; it swallows both the dirty and the clean. Have you not heard how so many children run away to the city and then change their names until their own mothers cannot recognize the seeds of their own wombs? Was it not Maringa who brought the story of a girl who slept with her own father whom she had left a long time ago? But when the father followed her, he flowed with the desires of the city, sleeping with every woman who said 'yes', until he ended up like the hen which ate its own eggs. Imagine, Marita, a man being his own son-in-law, his own grandfather, paying the bride-wealth to himself. Imagine the shame, Marita.

But Marita, you surprise me. Why did you choose to die like that? Why did you have to take the place of a pig, Marita? It is not good for a person to take the place of a pig. Did you not say that an eagle can never become a hen? Your own words, coming from those lips when the days you could smile were here. I have seen people's hands shivering when they cut the throat of a pig. I have seen little children with naked bellies crowding to watch their parents cut the cock's throat so that they eat good meat. But, Marita, do you not think that the children feel the knife in their own flesh as they stand there? Do you not think that shivering hands are feeling the pain in the man's heart? Marita, it is not good for someone like you to take the place of a pig. This is the truth, Marita, when a sharp knife cuts through a living thing, Marita, I feel the pain too. How can I not? I do not know why, but this is what happens.

17

But then you should not have died like that. You should have refused, refused just like that in the glare of the sun's eyes.

Marita, this place. Do you know what it is to listen to the many voices of the tractors roaring at the soil without you nearby? You were born here, Marita. But how could you now know what it was like to have shared this breath from the wind with you? to know that you smiled at the cowdung smoking fresh near the cows? to know that your heart shook too when thunder slapped my sides as I lay alone on the mat of my nights? to see your eyes glitter in answer to the singing of the birds running after each other in the sky? And you in front of me with the big water-pot sitting so well on your ruffled hair . . . 'My child, let us walk fast, the rains are near. Can't you see the birds flying in circles up there in the sky? What is that bird singing about? Hasn't your mother told you these things? Hurry child, when you see the ants moving in a long row like this, that is rain near us. The rains are just behind the hill. Ants are clever. They know when the rains are coming. But they are not proud like us. They tell us about the changes in the air so that we can plough our fields. Hurry, child. Never mind the water spilling on to your face. Do you not know that our ancestors said water should clean all other things since it was cleaner than anything they had ever known? It is only when water comes to the soil and meets people that it becomes dirty, carrying all sorts of things made by the hands of humans like you and me. Let us walk faster, child, there are many of my age-group who did not see this sun we see today because the rains did not allow them to do so. Shame on me, I must not mention such things when the clouds are already stretching their hands above us. Shame . . .'

Marita, you are the one who told me that the earth breathed, so I should not put dirt all over the place. The trees, the rocks, the soil, you said they once talked like people, they ran races and gave each other prizes. How I imagined the baobab running clumsily across the plains, with grass and the little trees laughing at the big belly of the baobab heaving up and down. Now that you are dead, Marita, who will tell me stories of lizards courting the girl in the next village, and tortoises going hunting for elephant and buffalo? The whole forest was full of things talking to each other when you were alive, Marita. But all I have to do now is to stare at the sky with your wounded face in my heart. Yes, I feel the warmth of the cowdung on my feet, but can that remove wells of tears that come out of my eyes every day? Why did you go alone, Marita? Did you not say that your own father once said the city was full of lions? Then how could you go to the forest of lions alone, without someone to warn you that a lion was coming from this forest or that, another eye to see the back which you cannot see with two eyes? Marita, listen to Manyepo shouting at the other women who have not finished weeding their daily portion. The words you used to say were that the women will one day break their backs weeding the fields of the white man. Things are still as they were when your feet walked here, Marita. These women will not have any back to use for playing with their husbands, you used to say, Marita. But you used to tell Manyepo that work with no rest was not good for the body, Marita. Now I do not know who will tell Manyepo those few things you used to tell him about us. The men are all castrated, you used to say. They cannot lift up their heads against one man who uses the baas boy as his whip.

. . . You women over there, stop gossiping about the latest love potions and get on with the work. You were not brought here to share your gossip with baas Manyepo. He brought you here to work. If you are too old to work, then say so and baas will get someone to take your place. Do not smile at me as if I am your husband. As for that woman with a terrorist for a son, she will one day feel the harshness of my arm, I tell you. You came here to look for work on your own and if you think baas persuades anybody to keep you here, you are dreaming. Baas knows all the things you do which you think your terrorist son will help you with. If you think you come here to fill the baas's forests with shit, then I tell you one day you will eat that shit yourself. That's why your husband wants baas to chase you from this farm. You must thank me for persuading baas to keep you for another few seasons . . .

But those are the insults you would not stand, Marita . . . What is the white man's loin-cloth saying today? Has the white man wetted his loin-cloth so much that it has the courage to drip

19

its wetness on us? Go away and listen to your baas's insults. Do you think we are stones to work without resting? If the white man has given you part of his poisonous drink, you must drink it bit by bit until the time you know how to control it. If you want us to control your drink for you, then we will tell you the words we tell to our small children when they wet their sleeping places . . . Marita, you were once fire itself, pure fire that ate into the heart of those who thought they were made of stone. You had to be that, Marita, otherwise you and my mother would not have had time to sleep in your own blankets working without rest for Manyepo. You see, Manyepo is another one with things in his head . . . My boy, *hini wena enza rapo masimu kamina?* Fucking stealing my mealie-cobs, and *mina bulala muntu lapa munyeskati* . . . But Manyepo, how can we steal your maize when we did not cut the lot while we were weeding? You must learn to be thankful, Manyepo. To give us a tin of beans is good, Manyepo, but look at what you eat. The cook in your own house is as fat as a baobab from eating the left-overs. What about what you eat yourself? It must be food even God has not known how it smells. Manyepo, why don't you look at your dogs and our dogs? Your dogs are fat as hippos while ours are blown away by the wind. If you want to know how well someone is living, just look at his dog. Then you wouldn't come here and say bad things about us who work to give you a good life, Manyepo . . .

Then your husband, Marita, would be called to Manyepo's house to be scolded like a child. And he would come back to you and spit in your eyes.

. . . Woman, since when have you become a man? If you are a witch, the white man is not afraid of witches. You will be dismissed here and not a calf will miss you. If you are dismissed, let me tell you that you will go alone. I am not going back to that reserve where dogs and people eat from one plate. The reserves are not even good for donkeys to live in. Now, if you go around shitting in people's wells, you must remember that the day they catch you, you will have to look for another village to settle in. Never mind all the work you do here, Manyepo will see to it that you are trimmed of those feathers which you boast of. Do you think all these people who shut their mouths in front of Manyepo are mere shadows of their fathers' children? They know who gives them their daily bread, I tell you. You must learn to shut your mouth if you still want to continue filling your belly with Manyepo's beans, that's all. Have your parents not told you that you must not quarrel with the midwife if you still want to bear more children? That is what you must do, Marita. If you shit in the village well, remember that tomorrow you will carry your water-pot that way for more water. Be careful about your footsteps, Marita, otherwise you will end up with your own toes covered in shit. Marita, you are a married woman, the sins of a married woman also smear on to her husband. That's why when they see a mad wife they always say the man is in big trouble, the man eats what even a dog has never eaten, the man has eaten the woman's thing. Do you want me to be like that, Marita? A man with a beard must control his wife. Not let her run around wild like a rabid dog. If you are determined to continue with this madness, you will see why the dog cannot laugh while it can show you its teeth. I tell you this because you are still my wife. But remember that there are many young girls looking for men like me with a good job and a good record with the white man on this farm . . .

And how you stared at him, Marita, as if the man had the wrong things coming out of his mouth instead of the other end. Marita, you do not know how it is to breathe the air without sharing it with you. You do not know how these trees will never give me the coolness which they gave us together as we sat there to listen to the words your son left us to go to the war. You did not mind when they called you Mother of Terrorists. You just smiled as if you were happy to bring forth children who would roast other children to eat. Children who were said to be so cruel they could throw a man into large flames to be consumed while they danced round the fire like the monsters you once told me about in the story of the girls who ran after man-lions without knowing it. But Marita, did you find your son, then?'

3 **Marume**

MANYEPO, look at my bare breast, and these cracked feet, do you not think that my feet should be covered so that I can work better in the muddy soil of your fields? All the children staring at a woman's bare breasts, do you not think it is shameful? Why do you not give your own wife that chance to go around half-naked with flies cleaning their coats on her nipples? As you say with that harsh mouth of yours . . . the work is not hard, even children can do it, you people are bone lazy . . . why do your own children only come to admire the green maize and not work with us in the fields for a day? These things are not good, Manyepo. My own wife has been telling you these things for a long time, but you dared call her wide-mouth. You even insulted her with her private parts in the presence of all the men and women of this farm. Do you think the girls in this farm will respect me when they hear the private parts of my own wife being mentioned in public? It is not good, Manyepo. I know my wife is full of harshness, but she works harder than any woman you have ever brought here to this farm. She works until she cannot sleep at night. She groans and says she has things crawling in her blood, things which she has asked Marume, the herbalist, to try to calm down. But she still complains, only at home in the compound. She says her blood will one day burst out and leave her dry. But she never tells you these things because she says you do not care. You only care to have your work done in the fields. They called you Manyepo because you think we are always lying to you. How can we be liars all of us except the baas boy? Was he not born in the same village as me? Did his father give him different rules from those which my father gave me before I went to herd cattle in the forest? You say we smell of things you do not understand, we lie, we are lazy as children and we should always have someone to make sure that we work, do you think we are children with all

23

this beard on our faces? Have we, the men, not made our wives pregnant and have the wives not become pregnant after we slept with them? Then how do you come to think that we are children, Manyepo? Men should be treated like men, Manyepo. But who told you that a man can be beaten just like that? To slap a man in the face in front of his own wife and children, Manyepo, do you know that it is like killing him?

But then listen to what Marita has said in my own ears today . . . Husband, you will have to remain alone. I want to go to the city to ask those who know, where my son is . . . You mean you want to go to the city alone, I say . . . Yes, because you cannot leave your white man, she says . . . But Marita, you are my wife I married with my own father's cattle, I tell her as she screeches the dry soil with her fingernails. She looks me in the face like a policeman arresting a thief. She is so bold that I can see her boldness in the eyes and on the face. She stares at me and tells me to take it as it is because she has already packed her belongings. She says she will not come back before she has found her son because they tell her that some lucky mothers have gone there and come out with their sons on the same bus. They say a long list, a very long line of names is hidden somewhere – where, if you are lucky to get someone who can read and who is full of patience, they can read the long list for you and tell you if your son is dead or not. They say many mothers have come out of that house with the names with hope that their children may still be walking on the soil in the city, but with different names from the ones the mothers gave them.

Marita wants to go and look for her son. She has been crying all the time, tears drowning her face all the time. Now she has made up her mind to go and see for herself . . . If the city is so frightening as you say, she says with a voice full of grief . . . why are so many people living there? . . . But Marita, do not be attracted by the many things people say about the city. What is bad will remain bad even if people say many good things about it. Look, Manyepo, she is going without even telling you

24

because she says you are not her father, but only you, my husband, must know about it so that people may not send bad wishes with me. She is going in a few days, Manyepo. But she does not fail to come to your fields to work harder than before, Manyepo. Do you know what it is to be a husband without a wife . . . all the cooking, washing for myself, carrying the water from the well over there? It's going to be very hard for me, let me tell you with my own mouth. Your own wife is all right because you have all the water and food you need prepared by Chisaga, that fat cook who sometimes puts all sorts of things in your food when you make him angry. Be careful, Manyepo. You must not make Chisaga angry. He will put dreadful things in your food and then watch you eat. It is bad, Manyepo, but I do not think I would not do it myself if you did the things you do to him, to me. I eat fire sometimes, but I have to control myself because my father taught me that even a chief's son is a commoner in other lands. In my own village you would not shake my beard the way you do here, Manyepo. I would have cut your throat a long time ago. But this humility is not empty-handed. A chief's son is a stranger, a commoner, in other lands. That is all.

You see Marita, there are too many shadows where we come from. Too many shadows . . . shadows, shadows without end. Think of it, I am standing under a tree, the tree decides to fall on me, crushing me to shreds, breaking my rib. Do you not remember the day the baas boy kept on saying that I was feigning pain, that there was nothing seriously wrong with me?

. . . Leave him for a while, but if Manyepo finds out, I will tell this man that he is a born liar. Tell your husband to rise and go to work. He did not come here to trouble us with all this feigned illness. How can a tree fall on someone just like that? He must have fallen from a rock, this your husband. You know how he spends much of his time hunting without Manyepo's permission, trapping animals all over the place. A man must learn to control the desires of his mouth, Marita. Your husband thinks life is easy. He wants to be taken in the baas's car to

25

the hospital, where does he think the baas makes time for that? Baas Manyepo is a good man, but we workers are the problem. We feign all sorts of things and think that he cannot understand our behaviour . . .

Marita, do you not see shadows in all this? Now you stand up to tell me you are going to look for your son in the city, leaving me alone to face Manyepo with a story, how do you think he will take it? I will be lucky to come out of it alive, Marita, alive. Remember how Chiriseri almost lost all his teeth when he went to tell Manyepo that his bull had been caught in the wire trap. Remember that, Marita. Marita, Manyepo can be fire itself. He eats fire and brings out the embers for the children to play with. I do not like him, but I have to work for him so that he can be happy. His happiness is my happiness. Think of me standing in front of his thick beard . . .

'Baas, Marita has disappeared. She has gone away without telling me, not even a word. She has taken all her things with her. I do not know when she will return, baas.'

'What do you mean, Marita has gone away? Are you not the husband?'

'I am the husband, baas, but she is a strong woman who thinks her own way, baas.'

'You must be joking. Tell me, how can she go when my fields need hard workers like her? You are organizing things behind my back, you pikinini. You want my farm to die, he e?'

'No baas, ask the baas boy, he knows the words which come out of Marita's mouth. Hot words without any care about how they will fall on the hearer's ears. I know nothing, baas.'

'You know nothing. Do you think I brought you here to know nothing? I know you think your terrorist son will one day appear here and cause trouble for me. Manyepo *chete*. I will fix him and bring you his testicles to eat. I am well armed, my boy. You will never run my farm through your intimidation. Ask the baas boy, I am as hot as fire itself if you mess around with me.'

Marita, these are the things you must think of. Flies will be

26

nibbling at my intestines very soon, Marita. It is not good for me, this thing you have started. Too many shadows in our life. It started long back, long, long back, Marita. I knew it from the way I ran away from school. Ask the baas boy. We were together in school, and I used to beat him up even in the forest fights we had when we herded cattle. But now he kicks me around like a small boy because he was able to stay at school much longer than me. He can write and speak the language of the white man. Did you not hear him the other day, even speaking through the nose like Manyepo? He is another one that one. The way he keeps on saying beg pardon, beg pardon, to Manyepo as if the white man were his own elder brother. Ask him, Marita, I left school just like that.

'Father, I have decided to stop going to the school.'

'What! You must be talking through the voice of some evil spirit. After I have just sold all my cattle so that you can go to school?'

'Since you like school so much, father, why don't you yourself go? I do not want to continue being whipped on the buttocks by a woman as if I were a small boy. A man like me must think of marrying and building a home, not waste time sitting doing nothing at the school.'

Then my father goes mad, picks up the firewood in the fireplace and tries to break my head with fire. I run away into the night full of fireflies, not fearing the howling of hyenas and jackals in the hills. I do not want to go to school, that is all. I stay in the forest for weeks, turning myself into a wild beast until my father feels pity for me and calls me back home. And now here I am, cracking my feet ploughing the land for another man and his wife to enjoy.

But Marita, do you think if it were not for these bad shadows, I would have done things like that? Even the way I married you, full of dark shadows. How can a man marry and then sleep with his wife for so long without making her pregnant? Poverty started fighting me a long time ago, Marita. Do you not re-

27

member the days all the people came to try to take you away to a medicine-man to see why you could not nourish the seed I planted in you? The woman's womb is dry, she ate all her eggs. The woman should give the man a chance, let him have another woman, then we will see if the nest continues to be empty. We cannot allow a name to die. The man cannot be buried with a rat. Yes, the man would have to be buried with a rat on his side if he dies without a child. Shame. That will be the end of the name. Childlessness is a sign of evil in the house. Evil spirits come in all sorts of ways. Have you not heard the story of a man who beat up his wife to death, to the grave? That is the work of the evil spirit. Evil spirits, they come in all sorts of ways. Some people just go away from home and never return as if they did not leave a name in the village. Evil spirits. Remember the man who slept with his own daughter and had a child . . . Marita these shadows seem to follow me wherever I go. I am the father of evil spirits. Shadows, and shadows . . . the way they tortured you with herbs and cuts all over your body to give you a new womb which would bear us children. 'If the river is flowing too strongly, flow with it,' you said. 'Flow to the very end because there you will find calmer waters so that you can swim to the bank,' you said with your own mouth. So now, if anybody asks me the name of one who has tasted all medicines in this land, I am not ashamed to mention your name. How could I continue to live in the same village? I packed my things and went away. Then when they gave you all sorts of names, you followed and we ended up in this forest where baas Manyepo is the chief. He growls for you to wake up, he growls for you to sleep, he growls for you to go and eat your afternoon meal, he growls for you to come and earn whatever he decides to give you. What can we do, Marita? We are chief's sons in a strange land.

28

4 Janifa

MARITA, how can you give me your pots and cooking things just like that? A woman giving away her pots and spoons is giving away her womanhood, my aunt used to say. Those are the marks of womanhood, Marita. How can you do such things to me? What will all the neighbours say when they hear that the things were given to a girl like me? The girl has been given the husband, the girl is the heir to a husband. Then they laugh as if they have seen what they have never seen before in their lives. Laughing at me all the time. It is not good to be the laughing stock of everybody in the farm. Farm people talk a lot. They say there is very little to talk about on the farm except Manyepo's latest victims, those he has beaten or kicked in front of their own wives or children. Do they not say he once beat up your husband because he does not have young children who would take over from you the work you are doing now? They even say Manyepo asked your husband to ask another man to sleep with you if he can't give you children himself. Do your ears not die when you hear such things about me? It is bad, Marita. Many bad things happen on this farm. Bad things even the ears of the deaf would not regret missing. You know how we wish we had wings when we see a bird flying in the air above the hills. But we never wish we had wings when we see a bird with a broken wing. It is the same, Marita.

'My girl, I am going to tell you what nobody else knows. It must not enter the ears of those whose tongues dance with stories.'

'What is it, Marita? Tell me. You know that it is you who said talk is the medicine for burdens of the heart.'

'I will leave my husband one of these days.'

'What? Leave a husband just like that? What has entered you? Do you not know that a man without a wife is like a leaf without a tree? Marita, talk properly.'

29

'Yes, I am leaving him tomorrow so that I go and look for my son in the city. They say some women have found their children and returned home happy. I want to be happy. I am not happy working for Manyepo. I tell him the problems of the workers here, he simply says Manyepo *kupela*. This time I want him to see that we are not liars. I take the bus tomorrow. You and my husband are the only two people who know. Although they say a secret is no longer a secret if it has touched the ears of two people, I have no quarrel with you, so whatever you do with what I have told you, it will not affect me, I will no longer be working for Manyepo. All he worries about is his work, nothing about me or my son. I have broken my back working for him, but all he is good at is pouring scorn on my husband because he thinks nobody will take my place when I get old. Do you think that talk can take us to sunset properly? But I have been keeping my mouth shut because I knew what I was thinking about. My thoughts are my own. So if you want to hear more, I will tell you if I pass through here with my son. They tell me there is a long piece of paper with all the names of those who died in Mozambique. So if my son's name is not there, I will know he is not dead. I will ask someone in the city to read the list to me. They say the city is full of people who can read even the languages from other places whose names I cannot say. They say there are good and bad people there just as we have them here. So I will persuade someone to read the names for me. I have a little money from breaking my back in Manyepo's fields, enough to give to some of those they say can read but do not have a job in the city. They will be tempted to do it for me because they tell me people can kill you if you refuse to give them some few coins. Since they like money more than people, I will tell them I have the money to give them if they can read the names for me. If they tell me that my son's name is not there, I will even give them some more.

'Do you know Chisaga? He is a good man but his greed for women is a bit too much. He came to me and pleaded that he will do anything if he can sleep with me. I said that was also my idea for a long time. But since he is the first to mention it, I want him to do something before he can sleep with me. I said he should steal some money for me from Manyepo's safe in the house where he cooks for him every day. Since Manyepo trusts him so much, he will not think it is him. Manyepo will think of other people who have been caught stealing his mangoes, but not Chisaga. So Chisaga has stolen the money for me. He expects to sleep with me when he is not working, one of these days. But he will have nobody to sleep with because I knew what I was doing. Do not open your mouth so much, child. The things men will do to satisfy the desire of their things are very surprising. Men will kill their own mothers if they stop them from satisfying the desires of their things. They can dig a hole through a mountain if you tell them you will be waiting the other side of the hill to give them your thing. Men are like children, my mother used to say. They rule everything, like children. Do they not say children are like kings? You let them play with fire, but you always keep looking. You always keep looking at them so that they do not burn their fingers. This is what we do all the time. Look and watch over them. If it were not for men, do you think your grandfather would have died in places where they could not return his body for burial? Did your mother not say that your grandfather died fighting a war started by a man called Hikila who wanted to rule the whole earth? Think of that, a man who does not even know how to cook for himself wants to rule the whole earth. That is what men are like. They look at their things erect in front of them and think they are kings. They do not know that it is just desire shooting out of them, nothing else. So child, you do what you can with the weaknesses of men, but do not let them play around with your body. It is your last property, you will die with it. So do not let people waste it like any rubbish they pick up in the image rubbish heap. I know this because my mouth has eaten medicines which even a dog would vomit. My ear has heard things even a witch would faint to hear . . .

'But if you do what you want to do, who will tell me the things that keep me here?' I say, amazed at how the chest of this one

31

woman contains so many mountains and valleys and dark holes.

But Marita, now that you are dead, who will show me where there are dark holes and stumps on the path to the well? Who will tell me the songs that made my heart sit in one place? Can you think of the hard hearts that are many here and tell me one which can lead me to a place of comfort? You used to say that a bird might fly high up in the sky, but its heart remains with the little ones in the nest. What I do not know is, am I one of the little ones you will think about as you fly in the sky?

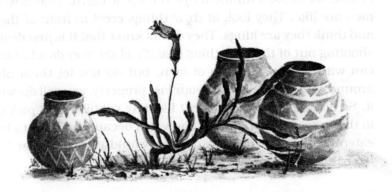

5 **Chisaga**

COOKING isn't a good thing for a man, not a man like me. But Marita thinks the job I do is the best on the farm. She thinks it is bad for a man to roam Manyepo's fields, smearing one's face with the black mud from the fields that stretch forever as if they were the sky. A man must do a job his children are proud to see him do, says Marita. Yes, I cook for Manyepo and his dogs, but what do I get in return . . . 'Thank you Chisaga, this was a good sauce, give some to the dog as well . . . Chisaga, what do the workers think of me? Do you talk much with them out there in the compound? . . . Tell me, Chisaga, what does your name mean in the village where you come from? Is it because you are big that they give you this name?. . . I am told Manyepo is a very respectable name, is that true? Do they call me Manyepo because I tell them when they are lazy? Bastards, there is not a farmer I know who does not have some form of nickname. Chisaga, what was your father's nickname? Did you see him, I mean were you born before he died? Shame'. . . I keep my mouth closed. Nothing beats a closed mouth, nothing. A closed mouth is a cave in which to hide. So I hide myself there so that Manyepo does not see too much in my mouth. Many people have killed themselves because they are too loud-mouthed. A loud mouth is a big trap. It can even kill lions. It burns forests. Did our people not say the tongue is a little flame which burns forests? Yes, it is true. So I have kept quiet for many years, they pass as if I do not see them in my own way, with my own eyes. Eyes that know much should always keep open. Manyepo, do you know what I could do with the food I cook for you? I could put a lot of things in your food. But I hate to think about it. If someone else did such things to my own food, I would never eat food again. Never. How can I eat food after it has been tainted with mucus or even water from the nappies. That is bad for anybody's mouth. As for the stomach, although they say a stomach is like a blind man, it can hold on to anything, it must not have unmentionable things in it. One's stomach is one's ancestor. Where would one be without a good stomach? Do they not say that one day, mouth, stomach, hand and foot engaged in a senseless argument about who was king? But when nose discovered the argument, he also refused to smell the food for them. Things could not work out well for the stomach. The eyes began to cry and the hands became weak, so weak that a mere fly could have made them collapse. Then an agreement was reached, and all worked well then. But stomach kept on rumbling and roaring like a lion to make sure that all kept hearing stomach's presence. This is why mouth thought of the saying that one's stomach is one's ancestor. Manyepo, know what is good for you, always.

'Chisaga, you bloody crook, too quiet for nothing.'

'Yes baas.'

'Yes baas, yes baas, can't you say something more than yes baas? Bring us the whisky quick, the madam is burning of thirst.'

'Yes baas.'

Manyepo, do you not know that the poor also see the rich? I may not be able to move it, but when a river flows near my crops, I see it. Some things are for the mouth, Manyepo. Other things are for the eyes only. A river cannot flow for ever. Seasons leave room for one another. Rain, dry, cold, rain, dry, cold, rain dry cold. Look at me now, poverty is like my stubborn friend. Always with me, but I look with the eyes of my own village and say – the leaves fall, but they will come back again one day. The stars die, but one day they will come back after the sun, their enemy, has left the dancing arena. Look at me. Do you think I do not dream of riding in a car like yours which flows like water in the river? A car that makes you sink into it as if you were in the depth of the waters without drowning. But recall the words of the ancestors. A king's son is a nobody in other lands, strange lands. So I just look at all this and swallow my saliva as if it has become a crime to spit it on to the hard earth.

Yes, Marita, I have been wanting to sleep with you for a long time. I have been wanting to see how I can help you for a long time. A very long time. A man must see things for a long time, only to say them out after a long time so that the heart can sift the chaff from the grain of the matter. Things must not be left to the clouds. But now that you also say you have been thinking about that for a long time, it makes me feel the place where my heart is stored. It makes me sing on my way home like the little girl who has heard words of love for the first time from the boy next door. But to take Manyepo's money is a job I have never dreamt of . . . Do not steal. The products of your arms are the things your heart should strive for . . . my own father used to say when I stole an egg or two from the chickens roaming the village . . . Use your hands, and be proud only of the products of your own hands . . . he used to say, staring at his empty hands, dry shrivelled hands that he had worn out working in the mines in Jo'burg. Joni . . . Joni is the place of all sorts of things . . . he said . . . the place where some men's sons went and never remembered to come back. Some even forgot their very names . . . Who is your father? the others asked . . . Why you bloody ask me who my father is? Do you not know that a man such as me cannot be born of man and woman? they answered back, staggering home in the mystery of the knives and all sorts of dangerous weapons . . . My father still came back with his head right. 'Trust the yields of your own hands,' he said. He died poor. Not a good thing for a man with so many children. Maybe if one is poor, one cannot afford to be poor in the head. So he died poor. A poor man. A poor man with a shrunken skin and a missing toe. The mines can do a lot of things to you which are difficult to describe. Many things.

This is why Marita says the job I do on this farm is good. I cannot have many accidents, except one day when I burnt the soup and the madam screamed as if I had put poison in the whole thing. Then trouble started until baas had to send me on a holiday for three months. I thought I would never come back to work for Manyepo again. When I came back I swallowed some saliva and spat a little bit on the shiny floor of the house to repent my sins. Many years have passed between those dangerous things and now. I am here and everybody is now happy that I am here. Baas drinks until he cannot say my name properly, all in my own eyes. Did he not once send me away before he started drinking? Then what happened? Manyepo started asking me to remain for the night so that I could fetch him the drinks. He drank the beer that burns the lungs until he could not walk, until his legs were made of water, then walking became as difficult as lifting an elephant. Very difficult. And I lifted him with my own arms and put him into his bed like a child. I did it, with my own arms. From that time, he scolds me with a smile on his face, he does not scold me too much about my drinking and singing in the farm compound. He just jokes about it, calls my mother a few names and asks for his food. Just like that. And he tells me secrets about how my people and I are lucky to be allowed several wives. If one woman is not good, then we can always go and sleep with the other. He calls it fucking, but he does not want to tell me what it means. Fucking boys, fucking girls, fucking lazy, fucking everything. I do not know what it all means, but I know it is not good to say it when Manyepo's wife is near. A stream does not flow forever. Marita, I smell your body all the time in my sleep. What can I do without saying your name on my lips? Let me do what you asked me to do, then I will see whether your words are full of weight. Words have weight, Marita. Words from a child's mouth are like feathers, real feathers. They fall on the lips and are blown away by the wind. Words with strength do not suffer the night's dew. They remain on their legs even after a storm has passed. Let your words be like the mountains which I found the same age when I was born and still they are full of power, standing there all the time doing the same things. Words must be like that, erect like the thing of a little boy on waking up, promising the girls that when I grow up certain things will happen which are being made now. That is what strong words are about, Marita. A stream does not flow for ever, but the stream remains there. It may dry, but it remains there like the hills which I saw when I was a little boy. All those rocks, big boulders and humps. I went over them, running up and down into the water that licked my bare soles. Then I jumped into the pools, naked as a baby, to feel the coolness running all over my body. Then I lay on the white rock spread there before me like a hard mat, feeling the pricking sun's sting eating into my shiny skin. It was like being a chief enjoying the leisures of my own land. Then I ran after the lizards, cutting their tails with a whip. But they always grew new tails like small plants cut when they were still keen to bloom with flowers. Yes, they grew new tails in a short time. And how I thought if someone cut off my own legs or hands, they would grow anew like tails of the lizards. It was such a joy, but soon I had to go to the forest to herd cattle and goats, running after the warm traces of cowdung smoking in the plains or mixed up in the water that I used to wash. Marita, the growling of the bull's stomach was something to me. I used to watch the cattle chewing lazily under the shade of the *musuma* trees, chewing as if to show me that I was not able to enjoy what they enjoyed. And the smell of the chewed grass, it told me who I was. And the smell of milk from the udder of the cows was such joy. Sometimes I wished I were a calf, but then I would get furious when I thought that my milk was taken away from my mother to be given away to the children of those who walk on two legs. Imagine, taking away the milk from a little calf to give your own children, that is good for the children who receive the milk, but the children whose milk is taken away do have pains in their hearts. It is not good. Marita, those hills, these memories remain here for ever. Your words must remain as permanent as the rocks and the hills, as the smell of cowdung or even the growling of the bull's stomach. It must be like that. Words must remain licking the soles of the feet of my memory so that I will do what I want to do without feeling bad. How can a man refuse what he has been offered? Do not refuse what you have been offered unless you are sure you will never receive anything good from the one who offers you. Even when you are given a snake, take it and throw it away later when you are alone. A gift should never be turned away. Take it, examine it, then see what you can do with it. If you can't do anything with it, throw it away when the giver has gone so that he will continue to think you are worth some more gifts. But I would be a fool to refuse sharing my blood with you. I have always desired to do so, but there are things which take a long time to be said because they should not fall on too many ears. They should fall only on the ears of those who must hear them. A thing like this, Marita, is not something you can go about shouting to all ears in the compound. It is not good. It is not good because your husband will eat me like a lion eating a little goat. It does not help to fight back when you know how much you deserve to be beaten. The thing will wear heavily on my heart until I die a bad death in my old age. Do they not say that those who have done bad things of regret do not die early? They live for a long time so that they can tell their children and the children of their children's children how ashamed they are of themselves. It is very painful to hear the fading voice of an old man rumbling on about how he did this or that without knowing that it was bad and that it could bring a dark cloud to his life . . . you see those young leaves sprouting with colour and smell, you see the young goats roaming among the rocks and taking large gourds of milk from the breasts of their own mother goats, I was like that myself until one day the earth turned its back on me. Then I spilled ancestral beer in the village well and finished the whole job by shitting in the well where I knew everybody came to fetch water. Then I laughed as old men and women vomited after drinking the bad things that came out of the body of a person . . . that was what my ears heard in their youth, from the mouth of the old man who wore skins because the earth had turned away from him . . . Earth, sky, I look at you and think what you have seen. You have seen many things, but you still keep quiet as if you had seen nothing. The things of inside the chest can burn one to death. They are heavy most of the time, Marita.

Manyepo is not a bad man, Marita. When you climb a tree you must not then tell it that its branches are bad when you are up there. It will let you fall to the ground where you came from like a stone. Then all the bones inside will break like the firewood we break to cook our own food. The tree will smile at your death as they bury you inside the fingers of the tree which take food for the leaves. Then the leaves will be green – even in the dry season – with the fat from a body that is buried there. Manyepo takes us as children without homes of our own because we came here to look for him on his farm. Do you not remember how the whole Muramba village came here to look for work when they heard a new farmer was coming to open a new farm? Some came with their children, their dogs and cats and all they could carry. Manyepo was here, fuming as if the villagers had annoyed him by coming to offer their sweat to him. He growled like a lion with little ones . . . Yes, what are you looking for, fools? Did someone say I was opening a refugee camp? Look at you, with dogs and cats and children. I want workers, not refugees. People must learn to work, not to loiter around as if waiting for manna from heaven. I want strong men and women, not children, bloody children with no idea there is something called work . . . Then he inspected us like a police sergeant, feeling the strength of our muscles to see who was full of bones and who was full of watery muscles . . . You can join my workers, not you. You are okay, but I will have to test you. All the women will go weeding for two months before I can be satisfied. Then I will tell you who stays and who goes. That is my way of doing things. I don't want to keep lazy bones on this farm. I have finished . . . Then we all worked for months without pay to get Manyepo's word. Marita, you worked like a donkey, losing all your sleep so that you could stay on. Then everything worked well, and you could stay. Too bad for your husband. He was weak with disease but Manyepo told him he was pretending to be ill so that he could stay on the farm for nothing. You pleaded with Manyepo, kneeling before him as if he were your husband until Manyepo said yes. That was the way it should be. Then I saw that Manyepo was not a bad man. He has bad and good in him like all of us. But this is his own land. We are like children up the tree. We cannot blame the tree for its crooked leaves. The tree is the way it is, so we have to climb if we want the fruits.

Yes, Manyepo will kick you and shame you in front of your own

people. His anger can spill over into the fields and nobody understands him. But we have taken him as he is. Our own fool. Every village has its own fool. Every family has its own priest, but behind every priest there is a fool. Manyepo is our fool. He gives us food, but we have to work first. He is not like Makaza, the district commissioner, who comes in his land-rover to tell us that by the end of tomorrow we must move because he is building a road where we live. If we do not move, Makaza drives bulldozers over our grass huts with a smile on his face. Then after he has destroyed our homes he comes the next day on his horse, to ask for taxes. Makaza is mad, I tell you. His madness has never been seen in these parts. Manyepo is better because his madness only lasts for a day or two. Makaza's madness is like a stomach. You cannot take it off for a while. It stays on until he dies.

Marita, for many years Manyepo has believed everything I tell him. Do you remember how I would tell him that my aunt had died and that is why I could not come to work on time? He always laughed and then said I owned all the aunts in the world and he allowed me to continue work without losing my pay. Not the way he treats you and your husband, Marita. You lose one day of work, he makes you lose all your pay for the whole month. To me he is a good man. I do not know what is inside him most of the time because sometimes he speaks in a language I do not know. A rough language which makes saliva jump out of his mouth like bullets from a gun. You should see him speak with his friends when they come. He laughs and tells endless stories to them in the language I can never understand. All he says to me is Chisaga, get us something good, my friends are here. Then I run around like a boy, cleaning everything, cooking his favourite food before telling him that all is well. Then he tells me to go out and play while they eat. They eat hills of food, leaving some for the dogs even when I have given the dogs some good food. Sometimes I am lucky to get the left-over food for my children too. But not always, Marita. Good things cannot be done every day. One day is cloudy, the next is cloudy and rainy, but the next is plain naked sky. It is the same with Manyepo. One day he is fire, the next day he is ashes, but he is our fool. Let me take what I have never taken from him because of you. I know he will think it is the two men he dismissed from work after he found them giving bad things to his dogs. Muringi and Chatora, how could you give your shit to Manyepo's dogs? You even went round the compound saying a dog is a dog, give it shit it will eat it and ask for more. Muringi, a man with children must not enjoy doing the things children do. Have you not heard Manyepo saying we are liars, we lie like children all the time? It is not good for a man like me, with children filling the compound, to be called a boy. But it is you, Muringi and Chatora, who make us look like children in the village. How do you expect Manyepo to resist whipping you as he did before he sent you away to the police. The police are not a thing to play with. They say they give them strong medicines to make them full of power and courage. Look what they did to you. They whipped you in the eyes of everyone like schoolchildren who have stolen from the teacher's garden. Now you have no work and the story of what you did has filled the ears of all who could give you a job. We must be careful, because the things of life need care.

6 Janifa

'MARITA, what will you do if you find your son?'

'Child, how can you ask me such a question?'

'Chokwadi, I want to know what you will do when you find your son.'

'I will be happy.'

'Just that?'

'Yes. Just that. The things that trouble my heart will go away. I will be happy.'

'But you are happy without him, Marita.'

'The things inside the heart are heavy, child. Very heavy.'

'You think he will want to marry me? That is what he wanted when he was little.'

'That is not for me to say. Days change all the time. But I will not be unhappy if you do not like him. The forest where he has now grown up for part of his life can make people change. Did you not hear what they said about those things which the fighters can do? I do not think they tell the truth all the time, but we would have to see with our own eyes to believe some of these things. The womb bears all sorts of people, thieves and priests. But I did not teach my child to do bad things because to do so is to shame myself in the whole village. How could he then leave me and start stealing, doing all dark things which the mouth is ashamed to name? This is why I also want to find him. I want to ask him if it is true, those things we heard once happened. It might be true as in the stories which our grandparents told us . . . . the stories of long-toothed ogres which feasted on the blood of good people until there were no good people remaining. Big monsters which ate fire and vomited the embers. It may be true that children can do all sorts of things. Did Muringi and Chatora not give Manyepo's dogs heaps of dung to prove that a dog is a dog, give it shit and it will eat and ask for more? You may call it madness, but it happens. But there are things that cannot happen. Dogs

43

eating shit is nothing new, but children eating their fathers is something that needs to be looked into by a strong medicine-man.

'So you think medicine-men can help?'

'Medicine-men of these days can cheat you into poverty. Do not trust them. They give us all sorts of roots and mixtures and claim we will be this or that, lies.'

'Then what does one do when children are said to eat their parents, roasting them just like that?'

'First see them do it before you join the hunt for the medicine-man. People are liars, know that.'

'But how can someone cook such a lie and have no shame going around telling it to the whole village?'

'Evil spirits still possess people, even those who have learnt the ways of the white man. Have you not seen how Manyepo swells with evil when his fields are not giving him what he has dreamt they would? Evil is all over the place.'

'Marita, you must join those who preach the new light of god. You will do well.'

'Why?'

'Because you are good with words.'

'You want me to join those mad ones who never end their talking until someone drops a coin in their bowl? My mother always told me to eat of my own sweat, not to beg like that.'

'Suppose you find that your son is one of those who talk of god and the power he has to move mountains from one place to another.'

'Do not fill your head with that rubbish. If god is so good and so full of power, why does he let the children of the compound workers die every day while Manyepo's children will never know what hunger and disease are all about? What crime did the little ones commit? The sins of the fathers and mothers, the preachers say.'

'Show me someone whose father or mother did not commit sin.'

'Marita, these things will trouble you for a long time. Is that why you refused to be washed with the holy water so that you would have more children?'

44

'Washing my belly with water so that I can have children, that is enough even to make the chickens laugh aloud.'

Marita, she is like that, a gentle fire which burns all the time. I do not know what I will do without her on this farm. Do you know that she works for me as well? When the baas boy gives me my small plot to weed, Marita quickly finishes my small bit and then goes to weed her own share. Child, what are you doing in these fields from which you will never harvest anything? You should be in school so that you do not end up in the same grave that will swallow your mother and me. I feel sad for you to think that Manyepo wants you to take your mother's place in the fields. We have better things to look forward to, child. Not this endless suffering. You were not born to suffer, child. The sun shines for everybody . . . then she wipes her face with a dirty palm, smearing her face just like that without caring. After the day's work, Marita looks like a ghost in the fields. Manyepo calls it hard work, but to think that Marita only gets a cup of beans for her food because she does not have children, it pains me inside. The things of inside are difficult to understand all the time. The things of inside burn like a strong fire, but I only look at Marita and the fire inside me stops burning me to death.

7 **The Spirits Speak**

1897 MY BONES FALL

ARISE my children. Do you not see the vultures flying over the corpses that are not yet? See the clouds which fake the flight of the vultures. Many clouds hiding many vultures with large beaks, all waiting for the many corpses that are not yet. Do you not see corpses when there are vultures in the sky? Look at the sky and tell me if you can see the sun? The large wings of the vultures are like shady clouds so that you cannot read the pattern of the sky. The sky, so old and with so many eyes that you do not see. But it remains silent all the time as if it were a blind puppy which does not know the colour of sunshine. The sky remains silent all the time as if it doesn't see anything on that earth. Look at the many wounds coming from the vultures, my children.

Disease has eaten into the wealth of your soil. Disease has eaten into the wills of your ancestors, your own fathers and mothers. Disease has sucked the juice of the land you inherited for your children. Do not sit and drink to the comfort of your hearts because there is no reason for you not to rise, not to see the clouds of vultures in the sky. Disease crawls on the rocks which you have known to sit there all the time for your protection. It has eaten into the core of the heart of the hard *mupani* and the great baobab. Disease grazes the pastures like the cattle of your wealth. Disease flies in the sky like the fish-eagle that heralds the coming of the season of the rains. Do not let the eyes of disease inflict its pain on the land while you sit under the shade of the tree without a name as if all was well. No, you cannot be children without parents to warn them that fire burns.

Disease comes like a swarm of white locusts covering the trees, breaking the branches with their weight, a weight never seen by any eyes alive today. The locusts of disease will eat into the fields of our harvests until we remain like orphans in the land we inherited of our children. We did not inherit this land for ourselves but for the children whom we have inside us. Look at the clouds of locusts. Eat them if your mouth waters for them, but this cannot be eaten since it is a bad omen. The locust that our ancestor says we can eat comes alone and runs away when we run after it. But this swarm cannot be on its own. It has its own messages which I tell you are not good. Have you ever seen a swarm of locusts so large and with such a mouth as to eat even the fireplace? Locusts that nibble and chew at everything, the hard *mupani* the succulent baobab, the hard rock? No. This is not a swarm to appease the eye of any ancestor. It is a swarm that would eat the children to death, goats and sheep to death. It is a swarm that cannot be measured. A swarm that does not spare even the well. Look what has happened to the fields and the forests. They are a mountain of white locusts.

But what does this tell us? What does the disease that the cattle have tell us? The disease that eats into the mouth of the cattle and goats and the donkeys. It does not tell us to sit and wait for other things to happen. It tells us that the clouds have changed in the manner they used to bring rain to us. When rain falls from earth to sky, we must know that things have begun to happen. Things we cannot understand. It is a sign that the sky has been tampered with. Bad hands are in it. Bad hands are inside the whole story. So we cannot wait to see what has to happen. He who waits while a murderer kills his own mother may not be able to live to tell the story to those who come later. The disease of the cattle and the goats is here, eating the cattle to death. Now, look at the bones littered on the plains. Does that look like a sign of good harvests to come? Does that look like signs for a successful hunt? Does that look like the year of the big *suma* harvest when the women went to the forest and came back with basketfuls of *suma*? I do not know, but let me tell you that to remain silent after seeing all those signs is to wait for my own end. An end so big it will be told by old men and women with wrinkles on their faces. And it will be sung by angry warriors in the forest, hunting but not even meeting the little rodents which are not hard to find. There is disease on the land. Disease spreads on the land like a mat, with everybody seeing it and not wanting to shout it to the whole village. Disease spreads with the coming of those who have walked the land without knees. The people without knees have knelt and broken their legs on our land, so they will not leave to go to the land of their own fathers. They will sit and hunt the animals because they do not have a place to stay, skinning the animals. But since they have big guns, their hunt is going to be successful, so that those of us with a big desire for meat will go to them in hiding and ask for a piece or two of meat. Roast meat, bones, bits of offal. Then they will say since the meat is so nice and you do not have big guns for hunting it, we can stay here and teach you how to hunt. We can stay here and even show you how to kill all your enemies with the big guns which we are able to make. Then some of us will say, the big guns are the things we have been waiting for. The big guns are the things which we can use to rob all those who have robbed us before. The big guns are the things we can use to protect our totem, the biggest in the land. The big guns are the ones we can use to protect our chiefs and the shrines of our ancestors. Do you not know that when the enemy villages attack us they pass dirty water on the shrines of our ancestors? That will then have to stop if we have the big guns which fire with clouds of smoke. If you can make us some more of the big guns, then stay and we will give you a little plot so that you can farm if you want . . . There is disease in this land, spread like the cloud which you will want to see change to rain. A cloud that never rains, a cloud that tortures us all with no rain but shining with the pregnancy of rains all the time.

I will run to the shrines of our ancestors and speak these words. I will say your children have refused to listen. They have eaten the fat from the carcase killed by an enemy, so their mouths have been sealed for ever unless you give them the medicine to make them wake up from their lost dreams. I will say this is the last time someone will honour you properly at this shrine because the children of your children have succumbed to silence. The children of your children will for ever not bring any gifts to these shrines. All the holy shrines will be turned into fields and playgrounds because your children have eaten the silent tree. A more powerful medicine-man has come to defeat the herds you left for your children. So they will not tell the people without knees to leave them alone to honour the graves of their ancestors. They will join the strangers in singing the songs of their own doom. They wear the loin-cloth of the strangers so that they will not know how to wear the things of their own hands. They have stopped making praise-songs to the great deeds of their fathers. No. They sing praise-songs only to the deeds of the strangers whose songs they do not understand. All this they do because they are lost. They do not know any more the footpath to their own wells which they dug with their own hands. Punish them if you want, but they are still not beyond any help. A few of them can stand up to the deeds of the strangers, because the strangers are not many yet. Some of them have gone to fetch their wives so that they can start multiplying in preparation for the long battle, the battle of many nights and days. So they do not want to say insulting things yet. They want to wait until they can fight. Do they not know that he who fights without enough preparation is throwing his only spear to the enemy?

They are clever, the strangers. They can say all the nice words of humility, but I see in their green eyes much mischief even as they go to give a few gifts to the king. The holy king accepts the gifts, but he says he knows the gifts he must accept and those he must not accept. He accepts because you told him that a gift must not be turned down. It must be accepted even if it is a useless gift from a child who does not know useful and worthless gifts. Even if it is a useless stick or the skin of an unripe fruit, it can be thrown away later when the giver has gone. So the holy king accepts the gifts from the stranger without knees.

But did Manyengavana not say that he heard the great king

boasting about the strange gifts he has been honoured with? Did he not even say in his own praise-song that he is the one who is feared by those whose knees only bend for him? That can only mean there is hidden happiness in the gifts the strangers have brought to the court of the great one. It can only mean while the mother does not think a little water brought by the little girl's spilling water-pot is useful, the mother has some pride in the child's achievement. What if one day the great king says the only gifts he will accept are those from the strangers? Will anyone move a tree which has been allowed to grow its roots under the rock? Will anyone be able to move the rock which has invited smaller rocks to sit on top of it.

✧

. . . I stood on the cliff of the mountain rock and saw the bones of my people falling like feathers from the bird high up in the sky. Who would save them crashing on to the hard soil, the hard rock beneath? . . .

✧

Arise all the bones of the land. Arise all the bones of the dying cattle. Arise all the bones of the locusts. Wield the power of the many bones scattered across the land and fight so that the land of the ancestors is not defiled by strange feet and strange hands. Do not allow the shrines of your fathers to wilt under the arms of the strangers who behave as if they do not have shrines where they come from. Do not let your ancestors be praised by tongues they do not understand. Rise and clean the sky if it cannot give you rains. Brew the beer of the ancestors and ask them to do what you cannot do. What sky will not listen to the thunderous voice of the ancestors? What cloud will not shed its tears to cool the earth when commanded by the thunderous voice of the ancestors? Rise all the insects of the land. Sing the many torturous tunes of the land so that any strange ears will know that an uprising is at hand. Rise you the colourful birds of the rivers and the hills. Sing all the tunes of the land so that any stranger will know that this land is the land of rising bones. Rise all the children of the land and refuse to suckle from strange breasts. Then all the strangers will know that the power of the land is more than the power of any other miracle that can cheat the eye.

The cattle are dead. The goats are dead. What will the herd boys do except to rise with all the creatures of the land? Where will they get the milk that kept them company in the forest? Only tears will keep them company. The disease of the land is here. The blood of the land flows on the lips of strangers, dripping with bits of flesh from the insides of the children. Rise and tell the ancestors that all the bringers of this evil will be made to tell the story of war and battle to their children. Rise. Rise. Rise. Rise you who look for honey in the forests. The land of the honey of the trees and the ant-hills is now diseased. Only tears flow there for the young and the old to rise and swell like boils on the buttocks of an elder.

In my sleep, I saw many clouds drifting from the south to the north. I saw clouds drifting from the place of sunset to the place of sunrise. I saw dark skies covered with clouds I did not know. Then I heard many voices of war, war-songs revived and war-songs made for the great fight of my people. Mothers, children, trees, insects, birds, animals, they all joined in the war-songs of the people. I saw many bones spread on large plains and on the hills. Bones spread like rough mats on the banks of the rivers and in the water. But the fish would not eat them. Rising bones. They spoke in many languages which I understood all. Tongues full of fire, not ashes. Clouds of bones rose from the scenes of many battles and engulfed the skies like many rain birds coming to greet the season. There were so many bones I could not count them. So many they made the sky rain with tears. Some I did not see where they were buried, but they leapt into the sky like a swarm of locusts, with such power that they broke the branches of the sky where they rested in their long journey to places I did not know. Right across the land of the rivers that flooded all the time, they heaved on the chest of the land until they formed one huge flood which trampled on the toes of armed strangers. Armed strangers who shot all the time for many days as if they were now hunting for ever. They shot into the hearts of the bones and kept on firing until they could not be seen in the smoke of their own gunpowder.

Then one sunset I saw them come together in a huge celebration of the success of their battle. They did not see the bones scattered on the battlefield. They sang in strange tongues which I could not understand, but they were songs of praise for their gods of war. They came from the celebration and bound all the survivors in heavy chains so that they will not rise again.

. . . you can torture me,
spread my bowels for the jackals to eat
and tear them to pieces,
mutilate my body with your anger,
throw my brains to the vultures,
leave the remains of my body in the playground
for your children to play with,
cut my ears to decorate your own ears,
cut my fingers
use them to wipe your own sweat . . .
my bones will rise in the spirit of war. They will
sing war-songs
with the fire of battle. They will compose new
war-songs and fight on
until the shrines of the land of their birth
are respected once more. My bones will rise
with such power
the graves will be too small
to contain them.
The ribs of the graves
will break when my bones rise,
and you stare in disbelief,
not knowing if your hunger for war
can stand up to it. Then the locusts will not be seen again
and strangers will not think that
he who accepts them is full of foolishness . . .

53

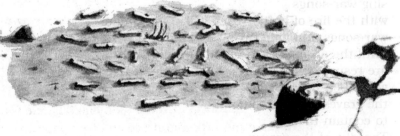

8 The Unknown Woman

MY BONES RISE AND FALL

'THE children have come, and they have been killed.

'What children, are you mad?'

'The children. They have been killed. But it has not been said what they wanted. They were killed.'

'Madness is eating into your thinking. How can you call armed gangsters, thieves, robbers, you call them the children? Whose children, if I might ask?'

'The children of the soil.'

'Listen to your evil Zapu spirit. Do you think a few armed gangsters will fight a whole army and win? You must be mad, raving mad. I am a government worker and I do not want to get mixed up in such things. Mine is to work and get home for a good day's rest, nothing else.'

'I did not say you must go and join them. After all, they have been killed.'

'I wish I could kill them myself. Then you will clean your head of all that rubbish about children. Meaning anybody who passes by armed with an old musket.'

'I did not say they are my children. Do you not know that even if you do not like them, they are someone's children?'

'And if I were that someone, I would wish I had never met the woman who kept those things in her stomach for nine full months. And if I hear you talk about the children again, you will die a bad death. I will report you to the police and they will come and tear you to pieces. Do you not remember how those you call children were torn to pieces before they even fired one shot from those dead guns they carried?'

'But even if they were killed, talking about them makes my blood move well. Do you want me to hide the things that make my blood move well? Then, what will I be, a corpse without any blood?'

'You and your corpses. I work at the hospital where there are so many corpses. You could borrow some if you wanted them for a day's company.'

'Yes, if the hospital has started killing people so that the corpses can be borrowed for a day's company, I would like to borrow one myself. Do you take me for a witch who would enjoy the company of a corpse? Do you take me for a witch, me, the daughter of Samanyanga whom you went to plead with in order for him to allow me to be your wife? Next time you must know which things hurt the heart of a woman when you speak.'

'If you do not shut up, I will call the police. They will know how to talk with you since you have such a tongue of fire.'

✧

We gave each other words of fire, I and my husband. I did not know that what is in the heart is in a deep cave. Why did you not tell me what you had done for all these years? I spent all the time feeling sorry for the hot words I had poured into your heart. But what did I know? Nothing. You hid the deeds that made many faces sad for many years. I did not know how it had all happened, but you hid it in the core of your heart like one hiding an old love affair with a neighbour's wife. Just like that. Leaving me to stay in the ignorance of the darkness of the night. What did I know about all these things which people told me at your death? Do you think it calms the heart of a woman to know after so many years that her husband had been having an affair with the wife of the neighbour? No, it disturbs the bottom of one's heart. It breaks the heart of the woman who gave birth to so many children who are your pride in all the beerhalls you visit. Did they not teach you that a man without boys to succeed him is a dead man? And did I not give you as many boys and girls as you had wished in your prayers? It does not matter, though. I did not wish to be compensated. I was doing my duty. But why did you not feel inside your heart that there were certain heavy things that I could have helped you

56

to carry? Yes, heavy things which need to be carried by two people. Old Sister Takunda tells me you saw the children before anybody else. Then you told them to go and hide behind some place so that you could bring the medicines under the cover of darkness. You never brought the medicines because you sneaked into the hands of the police and told them you saw an armed gang asking for medicines. They claimed they had come to fight the strangers, and you did not know who the strangers were. You were a government worker with all your life coming from the government. You did not want to play any tricks with the hand that fed you. So, can the police help to cleanse your hands? And the children were all killed.

But old Sister Takunda says there are others who had a different story. She says Old Mutambara, who was quite look-able then, met the children when he was hunting near the town. They stopped him and asked him if he knew a trust-worthy somebody who knew how to obtain medicines for them so that when they started fighting, they could treat themselves.

'No, I do not know any medicines, my children. Do not kill me. It is desire for buck meat which drives me into the forest like this. Nothing else. Do not point your guns at my chest. I have young children to raise and if I die now it will also be the death of the children. My wife is pregnant, and she has a weak chest. She will die now if I die.'

'No, baba, we are not murderers. Listen carefully to us. We are your children. All we need is medicine to treat ourselves if we should get injured in the fight with the strangers. Do you know someone who works near medicines? Someone who can take some medicines from where they are kept without being noticed for some time? That is all we need. One of us here will come with you to this someone so that we can talk with him ourselves. But it must be someone who keeps things in his chest.'

'But if you come with me with all your guns and things, the police will know. Mujoni Makaka is a wild one in this town. He will eat you up alive.'

'Easy, father. Let me change into better clothes. You can just call me the son of a relative visiting you from some far away place. Then all will be all right. No need for you to panic.'

Then when the young man came to you at the hospital, with Old Mutambara to tell you the new story, you told him to go and wait for you at the place of many ant-hills till you finish your afternoon shift. Then, on your way out, you would steal some medicines and bring them to the hiding place at night. But then what did the children get in place of the medicines? . . . many trucks of policemen and soldiers thirsting for blood. They say it took three days before they started shooting. They simply surrounded you like cattle so that you did not run away before they were ready with all they wanted to use to kill you. They say it was dirty the way you were killed. Soil mixed so easily with blood it was as if the sky was raining blood. All of you ended like vultures which had invaded the cattle in the village. And Makaka is said to have boasted that they should have come in their hundreds. Then all would have seen how much kaffir blood he could drink. Just like that. Boasting about the death of children who had come to cleanse the soil of the fatherland.

But Old Mutambara, why did you tell me this story on the death of my husband? Did you want me to be angry with a corpse? Such anger is useless, Mutambara. It is like anger against a child. What does it help to be angry with a child? Nothing. Look at me now, who will tell me exactly what happened, the way things actually happened? But it does not matter too much because the little I should know, I know now. Although they say every woman thinks her husband is the bringer of rain to the village, I do not know if I can believe that now. My ears have heard things which no tongue can say in the open.

9 Janifa

'WHAT is the bitch's name, ask her, in your language?'

'Marita. I work here in the fields. I am not a bitch.'

'For how long have you worked on this farm?'

'Many years. Many many years. From the time I was a girl as small as that one there. But I had a husband already.'

'How many children do you have?'

'Only one, ask my husband.'

'To hell with your husband, how many children do you have? I did not ask you if you have slept with a man.'

'True, only one, one boy.'

'Where is this one boy of yours?'

'I do not know. How can I know when he ran away from school with others and never came back.'

'Ran away from what, to where?'

'I do not know. He ran away from school.'

'And where did you think he ran away to?'

'How can I think anything about what I do not know?'

'Hey, I ask the questions, you answer them. Where did you think he ran away to?'

'They say other children have run away to another country so that they can come back with guns to fight. But I do not know if my child ran to that far away country too. I do not know. If I knew, I would have walked there myself to get him back to me. He is the only child I have.'

'Stop pleading for more children to me. I am not your ancestor, you understand?'

'Yes, he is the only child I have got. Nobody else. I got him after much travel in faraway places whose names I do not remember any more.'

'Take her for more serious interrogation, sergeant. She thinks we are her baas boy who howls at her so that she can

59

wake up to go to the fields. Take her for serious interrogation. She will talk straight.'

✧

Marita, how they brought you back torn like a piece of cloth. How they brought you back bleeding through the ears. It is difficult to kill a human being, Marita. I saw it with my own eyes. If you had been a goat or a dog, you would have been dead by the time they threw you naked on the muddy soil smelling of worms and cowdung. Watery soil that smelt of rotten roots and leaves. You lay there like one stabbed at the beer party fight. Do you remember how Rukato died at the compound? When I saw you there on the ground, I felt you were going to die like Rukato. You breathed, but the breath came out through frothy soil that had been pushed into your mouth. They had burnt you with burning things all over the body, even the places that cannot be mentioned. They had done things to you, things which people cannot do even to their rabid dogs which they do not want to come back. Bad things, Marita. Did you not say some of them must have tried to make you their wife? But you said you were only seeing darkness when that happened, so you were not sure that it actually happened. They kept you naked all the time, bringing even village boys to come and see all they wanted to see. Then they put a lot of other hard things through where you say children come from. Hard things which made you weak for many days. You could not even walk to behind the ant-hill to help yourself when the time came. You just sat there and told me you wanted to help yourself. It was all right with me, I did not mind. But some workers who did not like you because of your hard work mocked all the time. They said you were full of stupid stories about your child who was coming to kill the baas boy one day. They said that was why you did not listen or fear him.

If eyes could die after seeing bad things, mine would have died after seeing the way you were, Marita. All that blood from your ears, I felt my own heart draining away just like that. Heavy

60

things come out of our heart in such times Marita. Heavy things which words cannot name. Words are weak, Marita. Very weak. They fly in the wind like feathers. Feathers falling from a bird high up in the clouds. Have you not seen the hornbill fly in the wind? When the wind flows this way, the hornbill is taken from its own path in the air to another which the wind thinks is better. It is so because the hornbill has too many feathers. I hope someone plucks away some of them. It is like that with words. They float in the air like the hornbill on his journey through the path of air. How can I tell all those things you told? Things of strong men doing all sorts of things to a mere woman who does not know where the child of her own womb is. It is bad, but you always said bad things are part of good things. You said if there were no bad days then there would be no good days. I do not know how that is, but it sounds interesting to the heart with heavy things.

From the day they brought you back, Marita, I began to think you would never die. Only after a few days you asked me to accompany you to the well to fetch some water so that you could wash your wounds. You said they called you mother of the beasts, but you said it with a small flicker on your face. Does it mean you are happy to mother the beasts who roast children and eat them while their own parents sing and dance for the feast to go well? I do not understand a lot of things, Marita, but you made me know that I do not have to understand all things. Otherwise I would be God himself.

Now that you have gone away to places I do not know, I hear many voices calling after you. I hear voices of children asking for you to come back. I hear voices of ants as they walk up the path to the well, calling for you in silent whispers. I hear the birds telling me that you will not be there to see them run after one another before they lay the eggs in the nest up the tree of the ghosts. All those voices which tell me that your chest contained many things I will never understand. A chest must not contain too many things, you said once when I cried about my grandmother who had died before I was born. Every chest

61

has its own size, you said once when mother fainted after touching a snake in Manyepo's maize field. You even laughed at the smallness of the chest of a man who fainted only after seeing a lion which happened to be passing by without wanting to eat anybody. You said such chests usually are full of words so that when they tell stories, they tell them so well that anybody can believe them.

Today the sun has set. It will set again tomorrow. But you are not here to see it. That is the difference. Even the birds and the insects that sing, they sing the same way as they sang when you were here. But now that you are not here to hear them, that makes the difference. Suns will set, birds will sing, insects will sing, but the difference is in the ears that hear them. Today your ears are not here to hear them with me. Your blood is not here to tell me what all the songs of the forests of the farm say. So I wait for the time when the same things you taught me will be the same again. They say people die, but death does not say anything to those who have heard of it through gossip. It is like the smell of something bad. When you are told about the smell of a donkey that has died near the river, you always want to go and smell it for yourself. But when you get there, you hold your nose as if someone has dragged you to the place to make you suffer. Death is like that too.

I felt it when they brought you here half dead, smelling of real death blood, not the type of blood that comes from a goat's slit throat. That is the blood of meat, not the blood of death which I smelt from the wounds on Marita's body. So it is for many that are killed and the children smile at the knife eating into the body.

Did people not get sad when Rukato was stabbed to death? They did – but they said too that they hated his way of boasting about having slept with so-and-so's daughter or so-and-so's wife the day before . . . Yes, what can you do to me? I am Rukato the tree of many hooked thorns. Who can tackle the tree of many hooked thorns without dying? Try to tackle Rukato and only the neighbours will be able to tell their neighbours what a real corpse looks like . . . But when Rukato's corpse lay there like a bag of mealie-meal dropped from the tractor by Manyepo's driver, who did not hear their heart beat with sadness? Death is like that. Even if you wish it on someone, you may not be the one to see the corpse before anyone else . . .

'But Marita, do you remember the day the fighters came to the farm? They just arrived like sunrise, no guns, nothing.'

'You have heard about us, from dirty mouths full of hatred for us. Now we want to tell the story from our own side.'

'Yes, we have heard all sorts of bad things about you.'

'That we kill and eat children while their mothers look on?'

'Yes, and many more bad things.'

'That we rape daughters while their mothers dance *mhande*?'

'Yes, and many more bad things, very bad things which any mouth is ashamed to speak.'

'That we sleep with our own mothers and make them wives?'

'Yes, very bad things which make us think you are mad if all that is true.'

'Mother, I know it is not good for me to ask, but what is your name?'

'Marita.'

'Oh, the one they almost killed because your son ran away from the fire of the white man?'

'Yes, that is correct.'

'Who sold you out to the soldiers?'

'Who am I to know such things? All I would like to know is where my son is.'

'We see you are dying to see your son. The time will come when you can see your son from sunset to sunrise to sunset again. But now he is a people's soldier. The people sent him away to go and learn how to fight without running away as our ancestors did.'

'I wish I could believe you. Have you seen him with your own eyes or have you just heard that he is a fighter?'

'Who am I to see all the fighters? Only the ancestors have that power. I may not see them while I have a mouth because the mouth of a person cannot be trusted. It is not known when it will open because the mouth of a person opens even when the person is behind a bush helping himself. The mouth of a person sometimes has no shame.'

'I will believe you, my child. But my son was too small to carry a gun, any gun. The only thing he could carry was a bird sling for the birds.'

'He will grow, mother.'

'We will see when he returns.'

'Right, mother. Let us talk about more useful things which will take us up to sunset properly. How is the white farmer you are working for? Does he do bad things to you and other workers? Say it if he is evil and we will bring you his corpse in a short time. We have no time to waste. How is he? Does he call you such names as kaffir, boy, bobojani, skelemu?'

'His badness is just like any other person.'

'You mean he does not beat workers up like the other farmers we have visited?'

'He does not beat up workers for nothing. I said his badness is just like any other person's badness. It does not deserve to earn him death.'

'If you say so and nobody disagrees with you, mother, we shall leave you in peace.'

Marita, did I not see Manyepo kick you in the back as if you were a football? Did I not hear him curse at you, calling you all the bad things that the tongue can still mention and not rot? Marita, your heart surprises me.

'But Marita, why did you save Manyepo's life by lying like that?' I ask.

'Child, what do you think his mother will say when she hears that another woman sent her son to his death?'

'But Marita, did you not say that a tongue that lies will die a shameful death?'

'Yes, child, but it is better to let that tongue kill itself than to help it kill itself. The white man thinks we are children, that is why his tongue is loose. The day he learns that we are also grown-ups, he will learn to tighten his tongue. He was brought up like that. You do not expect him to think differently from what his mother told him. Do you think all of us here went to school where the white man is called baas: we were brought up like that. So it is not our fault. One day we will also learn that the white man is like us, if you prick him with a thorn in his buttocks, he will cry for his mother like anybody else.'

Marita, things of the heart are too many. Too many to know them all. Just too many. The heart cannot be filled. It will grow bigger and bigger all the time something is poured into it. It will grow bigger and bigger all the time.

✧

I saw footprints of the shiny bones. Then I felt the urge to find where they had been hidden. I walked endless sunny days in search of the smell that would lead me to where all the bones were gathered. Where are the scents from all the breaking pods of the trees, where are they so they can lead me to the bones of my people? Tell me, you who carry the weight of the earth, so that I can know and never forget. Sing to me the songs of the endless bones so that I may not be ashamed to follow the echoes of that endless song. Let the winds carry the echoes to the fields where I am working so that I will not say I ran after them. They may be mistaken for the voices of the winds, but I will know them when I hear even the echoes.

10 **The Unknown Woman**

A seed does not sleep in the soil for ever.
If it should, then a whole people is doomed
like the sun that refuses to rise.

A WOMAN, old and frail, walks through the heavy door of the
hospital, barefoot, unsure, her eyes roaming the place from the
shiny floor to the roof. She walks to the man sitting behind a
desk, pen in hand. He chews the other end of his pen, or sucks
it since most of his teeth are missing. He looks surprised, his
eyes seeming to accuse the other of intruding. It is as if a corpse
has walked right there in front of him, in daylight.

'I have come to take the body of the woman whose home is
not known by anybody,' she says, hesitant all the time. Her
dry lips quiver before they steady down with imposed confidence.

'What?'

'The body of the woman who is not known by anybody,' she
repeats in a soft plea. Her other hand gesturing to the man to
remind him that she is not in a hurry, but would like to see
the way of things quickly.

'I do not understand. Do you know her then?' he says,
dropping the pen on the desk.

'I do not know her, but someone ought to know her. How can
she not be known by someone in a big city like this one?'

'Anyway, who told you she was here? I mean, how did you
know she was here in the mortuary?'

'They say the radio said it. Then I saw it in the newspaper,
a big picture too,' the frail woman says with more confidence.

'Then you know her or someone who might know her,' the
man tries to reason.

'No, I don't know her much, but I know where she might come
from.'

67

'How did you know that? The woman had no papers or anything to identify her,' the man says in resignation.

'Her name is Marita, the one who had come to look for her son returning from the war. She is the one.'

'How do you know her? Come from the same place or something?'

'Boarded the same bus to the city when she came here. We talked a lot on the bus and she told me everything.'

'But you cannot take the body on those grounds. We need a relative with proof, something to show,' the man begins to feel hot inside himself.

'If nobody claims the body with proof, what will happen to the body?' she asks with a calm gesture of the arms and the head.

'Then government will take the body and bury it,' the man says.

'Then can I talk with government to give me the body so that I can bury it myself?' the woman insists.

'Government does not do it that way,' the man nibbles at the fingers of his left palm.

'Where does government stay so that I can visit him and ask for the body? I want the body, nothing else. I just want to take the body and bury it properly.' She winces as if in much pain.

'Mother, I think this has gone too far now. Can't you see I am losing my patience with your stupid request? How on earth do you expect to bury someone you have just met on a bus? Do you think burying someone is just like burying a cow or a donkey? Be reasonable!' He spits in between words, showers of anger burst through his teeth.

'If you want to scold me, I will not scold you back,' she mumbles softly.

'Look, I will not accept a mere witch like you coming here to such a big hospital just to cause trouble. Go and show your madness somewhere else or I will call the police.'

'You can speak like that if you have no mother, if you did not come from the womb of a mother like me. You can pour hot words out of your mouth, but you have a body in here which nobody wants to go and bury. I want to go and bury it because

68

I have seen the woman when she was alive.' She walks nearer to the man, prayerfully.

'I am sorry, mother, but tell me what makes you think you can bury someone whom you met on the bus? Tell me.' The man sits back and listens like a teacher attending to a child's plea.

Marita is not someone I met on the bus. She is much more than that. Imagine, just think of it, a woman who gives me so much of what is inside her heart without crying. In our journey she took me to the well, back into the kitchen, then to the forest to gather firewood. It does not happen every day that someone you meet shows you the pain inside her heart, the troubles inside her mind. The mind is a hidden thing. The heart also is a hidden thing. Do they not say the mouth is a small cave with which to hide the things of inside. Many burdensome things which weigh inside the breast of a person. Marita showed me all the burdens I have inside me, but she did so without shedding even a little tear or making me feel sorry for her.

From the time Marita sat beside me on the seat of the bus, I felt her warmth seep into me, tickling my heart with a certain joy inside. She just said, 'How high will the sun be by the time we get to the big city? I am anxious.' She stared at the country whirling away outside the bus, trees in their green and rocks wearing the different patterns of their birth, the grass green with little patches of bare ground as if the children have been playing there. But there were no children. These were large farmlands which nobody farms. The owners are frenzied or vicious when they see someone walking through these un-spoiled forests that are their farms. But there is no bus or car to take the walker away from the roads through the farms. So, one does not know how to leave the farmlands and reach the bus-stop. It is far away from the farm where I work,' she says with much ease, no bitterness.

69

But when we pass through the sugar farmlands, she keeps quiet as if she has nothing to say.

But then she says her own brother once worked there in the cane-fields. He did not return. They say he died of an unknown disease, so they could not allow us to take the body for burial at home in the way our ancestors taught us. The houses of the sugar plantations are not good for people who work so hard. You should see the cane-cutters rising early in the morning before anything is awake, and then see them return in the afternoon. They are like trees burnt black, with legs and eyes. You know they burn the cane before they cut it, to scare away big snakes, they say. But it turns the bodies of the cane-cutters black like charcoal. If you see your mother's son in that blackness, you cry. You cry just like that. Tears just come into your eyes, and your heart bleeds. Then you know that the only thing they will do to forget their pain is to drink much beer and end up singing empty songs about how things will be better tomorrow.

Do you think there will be a tomorrow for someone who is already dead today? Do you think that black ash is good for anybody's lungs? I do not think so. That is why my brother died a bad death. They say he was clever with the cane machete when he was still strong. He worked with a white man called baas Macdhogo, but they say the white man's temper was not good because he was getting old before he made much money, so he fought a lot with my brother until one day it happened. Then they came to us saying that he had died of something bad which can kill us all if we bury him – because we do not know how to prevent the sickness from spreading to the lungs of those near him. He will be buried by those who know how to stop the bad illness from spreading. We shut our mouths and said one day the sun will rise for all to see.

My friend, Marita says, I have these things in my heart, but the thing that swells inside like a boil is the desire to see my son alive again. He was only a boy when he left to go and fight for his people. Think of it, a young boy leaving to go and fight for his people just like that. Do you not know that there are many old people who did not even dream of fighting for their people when they were young? Old people whose knees weaken when the white people say come here or run there. But many young people of these days are not like that. I do not know what has become of the milk from the breasts of today's mothers. It must be very angry because it is only the young who are running away so that they can come back. Running away to come back like the sun. It runs away in darkness so that it can return with more light. My father said it runs away when the light inside finishes early: it runs away to the woman who has the flame stick which can be used to light it again. This is what the young people are doing.

But my sister, have you heard the stories people were spreading about the children when they came back? Some said their shoes pointed the other way when they are going one way. Some said their bodies were so strong the bullets of the soldiers did not go through their skins. All sorts of things like the one about how the fighters disappeared when the soldiers came. They said all the women became heavy with children, so when the soldiers came, they would not beat up pregnant women. After they left, all the women just passed some air and there the fighters were. Can you believe that? When you hear such things you begin to know that the heads of people are full of many things.

Marita, she tells stories as easily as she breathes. Just like that. Look at those rocks, my sister, Marita says. The story of how they came to stand like that is very interesting.

Your father must have told you the story when you were young. But the way the rocks stand there like bulls threatening you is very frightening. They say the white people take much time playing, climbing up the rocks and giving each other rewards for that. Such things should not be done for reward. Otherwise how do we give rewards to the one who made the rocks the way

71

they are? How can you give a reward for one who uses the axe instead of one who made the axe? The things white people do are very strange. They are like children in many ways. Do you know that Manyepo takes his gun when his head sends him to do so and goes to the forest to hunt? What does he do? He kills many animals and leaves them to rot in the forest. You might say he likes to leave meat for the jackals, but what does he have to do with jackals? And to leave all of it? It is very strange the way Manyepo does things. He does not even bring meat for the workers, no. He just kills many animals and takes a few pictures of them dying. Chisaga, the cook, says there are many pictures of elephants and kudu in Manyepo's house, hanging on the walls. If I were an ancestor, my sister, I would make him shoot himself one day so that he will know that death is a painful thing. The ancestors punish those who kill what they do not eat. Do you not know that a snake bites itself after receiving a small wound because it is in the habit of biting what it does not eat?

Behind those hills, Marita said, the earth turned red so that the people began to see blood all over the place. Even the trees grew red leaves smeared with blood. That is the land of the chief who accepts to eat a little of the left-overs from the white man's table. The chief was like that for many years until the fighters came to him and asked him if he himself was a left-over. The chief said, No, how can I be a left-over when I am a chief? They said he should have known that if one is a left-over, one eats left-overs. If he is not a left-over, why does he eat the left-overs of those everybody knows are wrong? Did the white people of the government not say that the people from the villages will not rule for one thousand years? Now, what makes you, chief, think that you do not come from the villages? Since you are a chief, is it not true that you are the leader of villagers? Then the chief panics when he sees the gun in the big coat which the fighter wears. He pleads with them, My children, do not kill me. I will not do it again. I am only eating what I can before I die. If I die before I eat everything which my appetite tells me to eat, I will not join the ancestors of my people. Let me try again because if I fail, I will come on my own and ask you to kill me the way you like. Please do not cut my head yet. I am a healthy man, and healthy people must not die.

The fighters leave him to go home without making any promises. Then after a few days of walking and seeing with their own eyes the poverty of the people, they decide they cannot wait much longer. The people did not have much to give to them. If the fighters do not feed, Marita says, they will stop fighting and go working in the fields. But they had seen so much poverty that it became harsh to their eyes. Let us leave, they said to each other. Let us look for better areas where there are fields that can give something to the farmers. Our hopes will die if we continue to see children dying every day and the cattle licking the soil as if it contains salt. We have learnt that we must free our people from poverty. Poverty is worse than war, they say. You can stop war through talking. You can't stop poverty through talking. So we must fight with all we have so that our people cannot continue to be buried in this ant-hill of poverty.

So the fighters moved on, but before they had gone very far, many aeroplanes coloured like leaves covered the whole sky like the locusts the old people still talk about. The aeroplanes made so much noise that the rocks shook and rolled down the hills. Then the aeroplanes surrounded the fighters, and many soldiers dropped from the sky like leaves, but with guns to kill all the fighters they could find. They came and shot like madmen, aiming at the goats, the fighters, the boulders, the trees, the air, everywhere. Then the fighters also fired their guns. The fight went on until the following day. But the fighters were not many, the soldiers were many. Do you know that it is easier to hit many people with a single stone than it is to hit one with one stone? The fighters died, many of them. But the soldiers died also. So many that the rocks and the trees were smeared with blood. Some of the flying machines fell to the ground, making such a big fire that many villagers could warm themselves even during the cold night, without anybody asking anybody to move this way and that way. It was very bad, many people dying like that. But it told the people that the fighters were not like anybody who is in this land visiting their relatives. Do you know that nobody was allowed to see those who had died? It was said that many lorries made many trips to carry dead bodies to a burial place. We never knew whose sons they were, but we knew that there would be much mourning in many villages. It was only after the rains had fallen that villagers were allowed to walk through the place. Many say the place still smells of death, so it is not a good place to pick firewood or to go to the bush to help yourself. Many of the few fighters died. It is said only two or three managed to run away with their lives. They came back after many months and said . . . that was war, that was the way to fight. Fight and run away so that you can wake up the following morning to try and come back and fight again. They said singers in far countries had sung songs, songs of running away and coming back to fight again. Fight again so that the fight is not finished until new fighters join to take over where it was left. The suffering of a fighter is a medal, they said. You, our parents, were told to baptize your children with water so that they can enter the kingdom of god. But we, the fighters of the land of our people, now tell you to baptize your children with the pain of war so that they can live to fight forever until the enemy surrenders. If you are taken and hit by the soldiers, do not think of giving up. Think that you have been given a medal to carry on the fight without fear. How can people fear death when they are dying slowly in poverty, disease and ignorance? A people that fears death will never enjoy freedom from the heavy chains of being called boys by people of the same age, men and women. To refuse to die for the motherland is to refuse to wear the medal of birth which gave us this land.

. . . So the fighters would speak long into the night so that those who are friendly with sleep would be struggling to hear a little of those things the fighters were saying.

Marita says all these things as if she was there. She says the fighters would never stop talking even if the meeting went on for a whole year. They always had new things to say. If they had nothing to say, they had something to sing. If they had nothing to sing, they had something to dance. It was such a fascinating thing that all the people began to think they also needed their own guns to go and kill the next white man. But the fighters said the fight was not with the white man, it was with the bad things he had in his palms. If a child has dirt in his palm, do we cut away his palm in order to get the dirt off it? No, we take the child, spank his bottom a little bit. If the child wants to eat the dirt, we take a stick to punish the child harder. If the child takes another stick to fight back, we then take a bigger stick and punish the child and overpower it. Now, the white man has refused to remove the dirt in his clenched fist. So we have to take a stick and whip the white man. One day the white man will say . . . Come my friends, you are not evil people. You are people who know the difference between dirt and cleanliness. Tell us what cleanliness is all about because we have stayed with dirt for many years without knowing that it was the dirt which stinks . . .

As Marita tells me these things her face winces, her eye flickers like a little flame. She tells me these things because she says, 'You people of the city do not know what war was all about.' She says, 'People of the city are spoilt with soft foods so they think that life is soft. People of the city look at their watches and then leave work without finishing any task. This is not so with people on the farms and the villages. They work until they finish this or that before they can catch the next meal. For people of the villages, to eat is to look for life, but for people of the towns, to eat is to look for something to do. The city is a wild place where many things lose purpose,' Marita tells me with a sternness that says I am part of her but I do not know what her life is all about. You know, Marita has hard palms which cannot crack easily. She has had a hard life. It does not shame her any more to take off her shoes in the bus. If the feet are painful, the shoes have to be removed. It does not need any explanation to anybody. But the people of the city first tell everybody that their toes are pricking them and can they take off their shoes without offending anybody? 'Can you think of it, sister?' Marita says. 'People of the city are strange. A lot has gone into their heads. So much has gone into their heads that to clean them is very difficult. Very difficult for anybody to do.'

Then, when we got to the city, Marita fell dumb just like that. She simply looked at the tall buildings and gasped for breath as if she was worrying about how to get her son. She only said, 'I will find him,' and shut her mouth as if all had been lost. She shut her mouth until she went wherever she went without saying a word to me. Then I saw what she had inside her chest. The things of inside the heart cannot be read by too many people. They burn inside like a big fire which people cannot know how to put out.

✧

If the birds and insects refused to sing, what would the forest be?

✧

'Can I take the body with me now? I have told you what nobody else knows, can I take the body of the woman whom nobody knows? The body of the woman whom nobody knows. It is bad not to be known by anyone in this big city.'

'Mother, I do not know how I can help you. I do not know how, honestly.'

The young man wipes away the tears in his eyes and looks the other way as if a bad wind has hit his face. His large head is sombre now, but the sun shines on both him and the frail old woman who sits there and pleads with him. She does not look at the sun or at the clock on the wall as he does. She sits there as if she is there to sit for ever and will never stand up. He utters something which she cannot hear properly, but she knows that talking does not help much. She knows that she has passed the stage of talking and quarrelling, but she will wait for an answer which she has come for, from the place where fighters were wiped off the face of the land because her husband had sold out on them. Innocent fighters, but she had only known that it was her husband who did it long after they had died, long after they had buried him too.

11 The Unknown Woman

THERE is a woman who sits patiently by the door of the house where they keep dead bodies so that they do not grow worms. Bad smells come out every time they open to bring out a new corpse or to take in another one. Bad smells which punch the face like the blow of a mad man. But the woman sits there, enduring. She waits for the corpse for which no one mourns. The one that is unmourned. Not those which someone knows. No. They are good corpses whose death has been watched by someone whose ear listened to the last words from those dying unmoving lips which even the flies avoid. She waits for the unmourned one inside the house where they keep corpses so that they do not grow worms. Worms are bad things. They come from nowhere and eat everything just like that. Even in the grave it is said worms will visit a corpse and eat it before they see there is nowhere to go. Worms are bad things. But there are some good ones which can make good food if you know how to cook them.

A truck full of men in colourless uniforms comes to a stop near the door of the house where they keep corpses so that worms do not grow inside them. A truck with clean-shaven men whose heads are as round as beans. Very round heads. They say bad things about people who die without anybody knowing them. They curse and spit, but their vulgar words do not escape her ears. She takes them as she has taken them before, without raising a finger or an eyebrow. It is as it should be. When a lion roars, ignore it and it will not maul you. Run away and it will be eating your insides before the neighbours are able to come to your rescue. Let them say what is within them, even without shame. When a mouth dances too much, know that what is there is not much. She gazes at them as if they are shadows of people from a bad dream. The flies on the door of the house where corpses are kept move. They know that they will have another chance to do what they have done before. The man with the keys to the house comes, walking carelessly without respect for the bodies inside. He says a few shameful words, but his eyes do not have either shame or fear for the dead.

'This woman is like a corpse, except that she is not yet cold,' he says, pointing at the woman sitting outside the house of corpses.

'What does she want?' asks the chief of the men who have come out of the truck with fenced windows.

'She says she wants the body which nobody knows, think of that. She claims the body as hers,' he chuckles as he vomits the story with much happiness.

'Soon she will have no body to claim because we have come to take the woman whose body nobody has claimed. We have orders from important people to take the body and bury it. We do it quickly because we have no time. The grave has already been dug, and we want to have the boys take the body, wrap it up in our type of blanket and bury it now. We are late as it is.'

'The woman says you cannot take the body because she is the only one who knows it. She says she wants to go to government to tell them she knows the body, would they give her permission to take it and bury it properly – whatever that means, I do not claim to know. But she has been sleeping here and spending the whole day here. We do not know what to do with her. When the police came to try to take her away, she threatened to strip naked. So they left her. They said she is not a violent woman, so there is no need to arrest her. Some day she will see that stubbornness does not pay. But do you know that a few people who take photographs came here and took pictures of her. I do not know what they will say because she did not say much. She simply said she wanted to take away the body of the woman whom nobody claimed to know for proper burial because she is the only one who knows the dead woman. It is strange what this independence of ours has brought into some people's heads. This stubbornness couldn't have been heard during the time of the white man's rule; the woman would be sitting in prison now, waiting for tomorrow morning. But now anybody can stand up and say they rule the piece of land on which they stand. Shit. Some of these people must have their heads chopped so that they will know that government is not a soaked chicken which they can just pick up and warm by the fireside.'

'Your mouth does not say much which is not true. Only ask my boys in there. Even our government can make you eat things which nobody would make you eat. Ask my boys in there. They have seen that when government says don't steal or kill, it should be so,' he says as he unlocks the fenced back door of the truck.

When the men come out with the body, a few people stand outside like spectators at a dance show. They point at the woman who has stood up to expose her frail body. Her breasts are not firm any more. She walks to the truck and climbs inside, seating herself in there as if all is well with her. A few people start talking about the madness they have seen in their short lives. There is no end to the types of madness, especially after this war which has eaten into the lives of everybody . . . It is very bad to see how some mad people stand in the middle of the street and eat newspapers as if they were eating delicious food. Have you seen how another mad man eats shoes by the corner of that street in the city? No, this is too much. To think that our government can just stand there and watch these people messing up the town, it is very bad. If I were the police I would arrest them all and imprison or hang them so that the city is not defiled. We are civilized people in this country. What do people from other countries say when they see all these people wearing rags in our streets? Near the railway station it is the worst. You would think the town is the headquarters for mad people from all the countries of the world . . . the man continues as he thinks everybody is listening to his fast tongue which has beaten all the other tongues in the competition. He does not see that some people have started moving away from him, pointing at his head and indicating circles in the air.

There, in the truck, the chief of those people who have come to bury Marita tries to persuade the woman to come out so that they can do what important people have said should be done. The woman threatens to scream and shout rape before she strips naked in front of them all. But the chief of the people in uniform insists that he does not take that type of behaviour, no, not even from some of those hard-headed people he keeps behind fences in the prison. But when he looks at his watch, he cocks his gun and threatens the woman in the truck. She bares her chest and asks him to be quick about it so that she can be buried in the same grave as Marita. The man is ashamed to shoot her just like that, so he slaps her in the face. That does not stop her from spitting in the face of the man. Anger swells in him as he breathes like a frog that has been left in the sun. He shouts to his men who are laughing as if they are the ones who invented laughter before anybody else. They laugh and mock him as his gun dangles in despair. He orders them to jump in . . . so that we can bury this prostitute alive with the corpse.

As the truck roars away, a few people take pictures and some write hurriedly in little books as if time had left them behind. The clouds in the sky also race west, following the power of the slowly setting sun. Dark clouds threaten heavy rain and a few deaths by lightning. But the leaves of the new trees of the city do not shake as wildly as the trees of the forests in the country-side. The cracked earth thirsts for more blood from the corpses from the house where they are kept. Even the few birds flying across the town know that the rains will come, but nothing yet seems to frighten them. They sing when the things inside them tell them to sing. They open their beaks when the beaks say they should be opened, maybe to swallow a little insect trying to visit its friends the other side of the kopje near the city.

12 **Chisaga**

MARITA, they say a woman rules in the land where Manyepo comes from. A woman with breasts like you. They say the husband of the woman wakes up every day to cook for her, wash her clothes and clean the plates. If you tell this story to the people in the village, they will die of laughter, Marita. They will laugh until they spill their gourds of beer and then scold you for telling such a big lie. A lie is a bad thing, Marita, but they do not know that a lie in one place can be the truth in another. That is the way life is. If you tell them that a man can call another man 'boy', they may not believe you, but those who have travelled will remind them that such stories are not new. I tell you with this mouth of mine, there are no new stories, only new ears for old stories. That is the way things are with me now. Marita, I have allowed you to rule the things that are inside me. Right inside me into the dregs of my own heart, the very dregs of the chest. Do they not say that only friends drink the dregs of a friend's beer pot? Although dregs are bad, many people are proud to drink them from a pot of beer. They say you can see the cleanliness of the pot from the colour of the dregs, then you know how clean your friend's wife is. Think of it, Marita, if one day in the dregs someone finds a lizard's tail, what would happen if dregs were not drunk by friends. The whole village would know. The man and his wife would fill conversations between quaffs of the seven-day brew. Even the women on the way to the well would have something to talk about. All sorts of things will come to the lips of those who have discovered a new tale. They will fatten the story until it is so fat that the owner of the story will not even know it. When tongues of the village start wagging, know that the wagging of the tails of dogs is nothing.

Marita, it is today that I have to sleep with you. Although a few

83

drops of rain have come, there is nothing else for me to think of. Look how I have washed and cleaned myself so that I smell the smells of the white man. I even took a few of the smelling things which Manyepo's wife uses so that you can see how far I am from the days when we came here to sell ourselves like cattle at the market. But let me not fill my heart with bad things when I know today I meet the woman whose eyes make everyone on this farm drunk with love. Even the neck of the woman sends many people stammering in their conversation with her. I do not talk of gossip. I talk of what I know, what I have seen with my own eyes. Did Manyepo not ask about you the other day as if you were his sister, with a drinking man's smile on his lips? I know inside him there is a strong desire to have you even in the fields. It is bad that you talk bad things with him all the time. Otherwise you would have come to work here in the house with me.

✧

'I called you here to ask one thing. What is this I hear about Marita running away last night? They tell me she has left all the things of her womanhood with you. The pots, the baskets, everything that makes a woman feel a woman.'

'Go and ask the one who told you those stories. All I can tell you is that I do not know where Marita has gone.'

'But do you think she can come back any day? Did she fight with her husband? Did Manyepo say some very bad things to her in the fields?'

'I do not know. I was not in the fields yesterday.'

'Who knows, then? Are you not her best friend on this farm? Since when have you learnt to hide so many things of your heart from the hearts of adults? You must talk because Man-yepo can eat fire and vomit the embers? Do not play with his anger especially when the rains are refusing to come down from the sky like this. Do you think he will care about skinning you alive and roasting the meat for his dogs? Keep quiet if you want to knock at the door of death. Keep quiet. When the time to talk comes, no one will ask you. You will sing it on your own in the fields for all to hear. You will tell even the *mupani* leaves

84

and the thorns out there so that they can help you to understand the anger of the man with no knees. If you think that our
ancestors were mad to call them the people without knees, you
will learn what that means soon. These people do not bend once
they have decided they will go straight. Have you not heard how
Manyepo went to kill a lion which had eaten his ox? He went
alone with his gun and the next day we heard the lion had been
killed. These people do not bend, I tell you. They will even cut
through a mountain if it is in their way to some place they want
to reach. Look how they have destroyed the mountain of the
ancestors. Someone told them there is much richness under
the mountain, the next day they had brought all sorts of things
to dig up the mountain. All the people with homes near there
were told to move to other places. The white man had no time
to tell them where those other places were because he wanted
to dig the mountain and get the wealth under it, nothing else.
So if you do not talk properly while I am here, when Manyepo
calls you, you will know that he does not bend like his
ancestors. A buck will bear a young one which is like itself even
in the manner of its walking. Manyepo is like that. You know
him.'

'What do you want me to tell you? Just say it and I will say
it after you. Do you have no shame talking to a young girl like
that? I am not even Marita's daughter, yet you want me to
speak like her daughter. Go and ask her husband if you want
to know. Husband and wife sleep together, so if Marita woke
up in the middle of the night, the husband will know where
she said she was going and when she would be back.'

'If you speak like that to me, you will soon know that anger
is one thing I am not short of. I can do what you can never
believe. I can forget whose daughter you are, I don't care. I have
done worse things before. Do not force me to do some more
now.'

'But I have not stolen or taken anything from you without
returning it. Why do you want to pour your anger on me like
that? I do not know what has entered you.'

'You can go before my anger spills on to the plates of the white
man, but know one thing. Marita left you all the things of her

85

womanhood. Know what that means. You can dream about
Marita, but know what Marita meant by leaving you all the
things of her kitchen. You can go. And if you should tell anybody that I have asked this, then I will find ways of closing
your mouth for ever. I am not in the habit of leaving crippled
monkeys to roam in my fields.'

❖

You stand in the shadow of the white man, Manyepo, his
tongue pouring anger at you for letting those rogues, Muringi
and Chatora, into his house to steal so much money. You stand
there and see streams of anger come out of the mouth that has
said worse things before. All the showers of hot saliva plaster
your face, and you only look, sometimes you lick and say to
your ancestors, why did you not fight the white man to the end?
How can a few people overpower the whole village? They had
guns, you will say, but what does it matter if they had guns?
If a gun killed many, there would still be many more to throw
a spear so that the enemy can be defeated. It is not easy to
defeat a man who is fighting to defend his homestead. Does
a man run away from his hut simply because a big snake has
been seen on the roof? A man must fight the snake until it
leaves his house or he kills it. To run away is to say to the snake,
you are king. You are king, so you can go ahead and rule. That
is not good for the ancestors. Any mother of such a person
would wish she had not had her breasts suckled by such a son.
Manyepo is pouring his anger on me all the time. He knows
I did not steal his money. He is sure of that, but he thinks I
helped Muringi and Chatora to hide in the bushes and sneak
in during the night to steal so much money. He says he is
thinking whether to keep on trusting me or not. Then the
moment he thinks trusting me is a bad thing, I will be out of
this farm just like that. To think that I can leave such a good
job to roam around in the country like an orphan is not a good
thing for me. To go again saying to unsmiling people, look at
me, I am a man who has cooked for Manyepo for many years,
but now he decided that I am no longer cooking good things

for him. That is bad. Who will allow me to work near their good things like Manyepo did to me? Nobody. I tell you, nobody.

But then what did I get out of it all? Does the preacher who came here not say things started going bad from the time a woman came to live together with a man? Things went very bad. The breast of a woman is too full of bad things. Too full with snakes and lizards which eat at her so that she does not have time to be a good person. I do not know what this will do for me, but Marita has put me in a hot pot of soup.

I know that people will say these are the wounds of one who wanted to get treatment from a herbalist. Such wounds are by choice. But Marita did not know that words must be filled with trust. She has roasted me like a sweet potato so that I can see the power of her breast. Now I am like a feather that flies to nowhere. I am the hornbill whose journey was disturbed by the wind. I am like the hornbill whose feathers make it look like a lot of meat. People know that it is only a heap of fluffy feathers, just feathers with nothing much inside. Not even enough meat for a child. The earth is ashamed to have me on it, filthy. But I will be there when stories of hidden things are mentioned. I will be there licking at the remains of the sun in me, nothing else. Just like a leaf blown by the wind from the tree up there where the leaves are made.

I will let my life drip like the last drops of the rain. But I cannot go back to the village to lick at the remains of the fat of the soil. That I cannot do. To start again choking from the endless smoke of the village, the dying children with swollen stomachs which make them look like small pregnant mothers. No. I would rather lift an elephant. Lift an elephant with a rhino as a cushion so that my head does not break. When a lion has been defeated, it goes away and promises to come back. It does not bite itself like a snake. I will look for the power that will make me come back without shame. Shame is a bad thing for a man to wear around. This is why they say that if you are seen by many people behind a bush, then it is better to change your totem and go to another village. Shame is nothing to be proud of. It cannot be displayed in the market for all to see. No one has ever volunteered to spread their shame by the roadside so that even children can touch and feel the warmth of shame. Do we not spend all our lives trying hard to hide our shame? This is the way it should be. Shame is not like sunshine. Nobody basks in it. Nobody asks to sit within it as if it were the dark shade of the tree. I know that when leaves fall, they are doing so that other new leaves may come, leaves of the same pattern, the same smell, but on different nodes. People will still sit on the same rocks enjoying the shade. I will be the leaf that returns to remind those who thought the leaf had died, that it is still alive, still high in the air near the fruit that is envied by every eye.

13 **Janifa**

MOTHER does not know the type of worm which has entered me since you flew away like a bird with a broken wing, like a dark cloud that refuses to let the belly of its rain come down. It does not matter now. It does not matter at all. I go to the places we went to together. I smell the smell of your sweat in each grain of sand you sat on. I crumble like the soil you warmed with the palm of your hands. Suns and suns come, many suns, but with the smell of many palms which you had. Palms for carrying the grain home. But all will be well. The rain grows weak inside me. Weak like the fly that has been poisoned together with the carcase. It does not make a difference, Marita. The warmth of a breast on the mouth of a baby or the sharpness of a knife on the throat of a goat. It does not make a difference. Rain or drought, it does not make a difference.

Things will change one day, Marita. A year does not come to sit where another one sat. It brings its own stool. It crawls at its own pace, not yesterday's pace, no. No. Look what Chisaga has done to me. My mother says women without children are bad worms, without wings to fly . . . My child, do not talk too much with Marita. She has holes in her stomach. She is barren land that cannot make seed become restless. The seed in her belly dries up and weeps to its death.

How can you talk with such a woman unless you want to inherit her barrenness? Only you should know that a pot without food in it may be useful, but given to a hungry man it is useless – like the rains which fall in the fields of a man who has not ploughed. Rain falls, thunder and the lightning cuts across the flesh of the sky, but what is it to a piece of land which no one ploughs . . . it is like that with Marita. So, mother says Marita speaks useless words which waste too many ears. Ears must not be wasted. There are only two of them for every head. Use them to listen to the howling of the wind and one day you will end up being blown away like the feathers of the hornbill. Do not listen to all that ears hunger for. Some words are the feathers of a dead bird which you do not bring home for a meal. Do you think your mother will thank you for bringing the head of an owl to the fireplace of your own people? An owl is an owl. You cannot call it anything in order for the meat in the pot to taste nice. A good mouth knows its own food, child. When a man chooses you to be his wife, he thinks you will know the food of his mouth . . .

Leave Marita alone. The flower that does not bloom should not gain credit because of the flower that blooms next to it. The white pumpkin invited the hungry eyes of the half-blind old woman to the darker one which is riper. Ripe, yes, ripe. Marita is not a tree you can lean on. She is not the fire where you can warm yourself happily because the firewood of her blood is not the firewood of good blood. To lean on her is to lean on a decaying stump . . . my mother says. Whenever her mouth opens, Marita is the meat that she chews. Marita is the dried meat of a bad animal that she chews. Think of it, Marita.

Marita, Chisaga did bad things to me. He said the pots and plates you left me spoke more than a child like me could understand. 'You will understand one day,' he said. 'A child does not know the sweetness of life until it sprouts a beard,' he said, as he munched the left-overs of the food from Manyepo's house. Manyepo gives him food which has been left after satisfying his own hunger. But Chisaga eats it as if it had been cooked by God. If God cooked anything, then we would have ashes for rain.

I laugh at all this, Marita, but I think my own mother was behind what Chisaga did to me. 'Go and fetch us some water,' she said, the corner of her eye glittering like a star torn away from the sky by the angry hand of God. 'Go and fetch us some water. Your father will wash very soon and there will be no water left to drink. Hurry up so that the sun does not get there first. Run like a child brought up by people. Run.' So I ran before the sun touched the tree near Manyepo's field of beans whose taste you know well. I ran because I was alone and the bird near the hill was beginning to howl the ominous song that you said means there is nothing good in life. Remember the bird with a head as sharp as a knife. That is the one. It sings those songs again these days. So I run, cutting the long shadows of the trees without doing them any harm. You know it is hard to injure a shadow, Marita. Shadows do not cry. Only people and birds cry, Marita. If other things cry, we do not know the language of their cry.

I run with all the power within me because darkness is full of things you cannot see. My heart says darkness is a bad thing because people say it is the blanket of evil. 'A dark husband is bad,' the women sing from the well, 'I might mistake him for the cooking pot.' You might laugh, Marita, but there are things which one must learn not to laugh at. It is like that.

On my way back, Marita, water dripping over my ears, licking my face like a little cat, I hear the movement of a small bush. I think it is the lizard thinking some small animal is after its tail. Then a little twig breaks like maize grain crackling in the hot pot. Then I see the shadow of a man with a beard that is learning to grow. I see him again following me. Then I think it is my eyes which are full of the things which many lips have told me for many years.

'Why do you walk on as if you cannot see me? It is me, the one you dream about always. Do not fear because I am the one you have always known will be your . . .'

'My what? Who are you?' I say with the fear welling up in me like Manyepo's dam filling up soon after the rains have died down.

'Did a woman not give you pots and other things which make a woman a woman?' he says, trying to hold my hand.

'Leave my hand alone,' I shout at him.

91

'You are not a child any more. Look at the boneless horns on your chest. Any man would take it as a gift from the ancestors to have you share your breath with him. Just listen to me and all our lives will be happiness. Happiness will flow in your father's house like a stream full with the rains. It will see light always, no darkness. Even the hard work which your parents do will melt away like the hailstones which melt soon after they have fallen.'

'I do not like what you are saying; maybe if you let me go things will be better for me. I know you cook for the white man, but to carry a gun does not mean you are a hunter. You and your wife can eat all the good things which the white man makes in his house but we have no hunger for such things. We eat what we can eat without any shame at all. So if you think that cooking for the white man makes my inside glow with envy, you are thinking wrong things.'

'Now listen to me. You make any noise and your body will be found in the dam after the dam has dried. You are my wife and I will sleep with you now. Do you not know what you and Marita did to make me miserable? I am the tree that never forgets its wounds while the axe sits at home smiling after a day of eating into the tree's flesh.'

Then I do not know what happened, Marita. The police came and took me to their camp, but my mother said, 'The man who did it is the child's friend. We like him, so do not put him in jail. The only problem is that the child felt the first pains of pleasure. That is why she came to tell you the story. We like Chisaga very much. He eats here every day. He is not a bad man . . .' so the police shook their heads and went to Manyepo. Manyepo threw his hands into the air with anger. 'My cook cannot do such things. Leave him alone or I will drive to the district commissioner. You catch Maringi and Chatora, the bastards have given enough trouble to my workers. You catch them and bring them here. I will castrate the bloody fools in front of everybody . . .' That was the end, Marita. That was the end of the hornbill's journey. The wind had taken the hornbill to the wrong destination. So I sit here alone with the wounds which my mother thinks will give me pleasure one day. Blood flowing all the time, hurting my inside as I think of the day they brought you, Marita, worn out with abuse, worn out like an old piece of cloth, torn inside, torn like a worthless thing that nobody cares about.

To the medicine-man, my mother said I had too many bad things in my head. She says my head is full of lizards, worms, snails, bad roots and half-moons. She says the things I say in my sleep must never be heard from the lips of one so young. Things that make the chest swell, the heart beat and the hair of the head move like the beard of a cat. She hears me sing songs only mad people sing, she says, songs that say the earth is bad, the trees talk to people but people do not listen, things never said by a healthy tongue . . . Give her some herbs to calm her mind, give her some herbs to steady her down so that she can grow up to be a good woman. It is a shame if a young woman like this grows up to be a flame in the village. The farm is not a good place for the illness which she has now. But what can we do, no one would choose to keep her in the village because all the relatives think my husband has used bad herbs on her so that he can get a better job on the farm. The things that workers will do to get favours from the baas boy. People are bad when they work for someone because they kill so many unknown things so that they can get favours. Some men sleep with their own mothers in order for things of the earth to favour them . . . she says. She thinks I ruin her nights because my head does not like darkness any more. In the dark I see many dark faces creeping towards me, coming as shadows to entice me to do bad things. But I won't let them do these bad things to me. I scream and shout so that all those near me can come and help me. I scream so that everybody can know the coals that are burning inside me. When fire burns inside a person, it must be put out. Put out the fire inside the chest, the fire that burns without being seen is dangerous. People will think all is well, all is flowing smoothly like the water of the big river, but if they listen closely they will hear the thunder that is there. But the darkness remains the darkness of one person. You

93

can't say to the hill go away and it goes away. The same with the darkness of the heart, you cannot tell it to go away with your mouth like that. So my mother thinks the herbs will help one day, many roots whose source I do not know. Bitter roots that I have to take so that I do not continue to die.

Marita, you told me sad stories of the wounds of your heart. Many wounds which no one can see. Wounds cut with big knives and machetes. I listened because I saw them. Now I have no one to listen to me. I have only the blood which I saw smeared on your black thighs. Thighs roughened with hard work in Manyepo's fields. A face stern, with stories found in the many cracks of the face. Did you not say every crack on the face of a farm worker is an endless story? Maybe it is good to have stories, but it is better to have people to share them with. I am young like a small maize plant; if a maize plant is alone in the forest, why does it not grow? Why does it not ripen like the tree in whose shadow it is growing? It cannot grow because it is alone. It has no one to talk to.

Tears are not water. They must not be seen every day. They are not water. The well of tears is not visited by anyone. No one knows the colour and shape of the well of tears. If tears are seen every day, things are bad inside, Marita. Things are bad. Dark things that eat you from inside until you grow as thin as me. They say there is a worm that wriggles inside the heart of troubles. The worm eats all the courage that is left so one cries all the time. To cry all the time is bad for the body. This is why people ask, 'What is wrong?' when you cry. 'Who has beaten you? Tell us who has beaten you so that we can go and beat him also.' It is not good to cry all the time, Marita. People say that much crying will soon mean death. Crying and death are friends, Marita. They are friends. Wherever crying is found, death is up the tree ready to jump down so that people can change the tune of their cry. Death is happy when people cry. Death smiles when he sees tears roll down the young cheeks of a girl who has suffered what Chisaga has done to me. Chisaga tore me to shreds, and all that bleeding just

94

because he wanted to satisfy his desires. I wanted to go and put poison in Chisaga's food, the white poison Manyepo uses to kill insects in his garden. But my heart said no, it might kill all the children from the smallest to the biggest. After all, Chisaga eats on the table of his baas. It is bad to be the way I am, Marita, but I still have time to think what to do. He sees me all the time and smiles his fat smile like a dog that has seen a bitch on heat. It is not good to hate and do nothing about it. It eats me inside like that thing which looks like a rat but is too blind to come out to look for food, so it eats the soil underneath. It eats the soil until the ground is full of holes. This is what it is, Marita.

'Mother, why did you take me to the herbalist?' I ask again and again. But mother would not listen to me. She screams and says I know more than I should know. 'Keep your mouth shut.'

'But the herbalist is a bad man. Last time when you left me with him, he wanted to do bad things with me.'

'That is part of the treatment,' he says. But I tell him Chisaga did bad things to me, that is why I walk with much hardship. He laughs and says I will be all right, every woman has that once a month.

'Do not worry about that,' he chuckles as if it pleases him to see blood come out of me that way. Then after many days he sees that the blood comes out all the time, flowing until I am very weak. He gazes at me and says I am an evil woman who could kill a man any time. He asks me to go home alone since he cannot cure me properly.

'Try another herbalist,' he says. 'There are many herbalists in this part of the land.' He packs his roots and bones and goes to his wife's house, leaving me alone as if I have a bad smell which can kill his nostrils. And at night when I cry with loneliness, he comes to the door and burns a few herbs whose smell is disgusting. He says a few words in a language I do not know, then spits through the door and curses. Then I take courage and say to myself soon it will be day so that I can walk to my own mother even if the pain kills me on the way. Before sunrise I walk away from the house of bad roots and ominous bones so that I can see my own mother before I die. Later when he discovers that I have gone away, he runs to the village, shouting that his patient has escaped. 'Help me look for her. I do not know the kind of evil spirit in this one. I do not understand how such a vicious evil spirit can enter the soul of such a young girl. Come, help me look for her because when her mother comes here, I will not know how to tell her such a story,' he feverishly calls all the villagers.

Marita, it is sunset now, I hear the bones inside me creaking with the spirit of walking which is in me. They creak like the ribs of an old scotch-cart without grease. But I have to walk on until I can see my mother. I want to see her so that I can spit in her face before I leave her. She always thinks I am looking for a husband so that I can make grandchildren for her. This is why she sends me to all sorts of herbalists, cruel people who do not know the pain in me, the seeds of pain inside me. It is sunset, Marita. The smell of new leaves tells me that there are other things which are good. Even the birds which jump up and down from the nests of their little ones, they are my friends. They give me the power to go on so that I can spit on the face of my mother. As for my father, his head is numb all the time. Whenever he wants to say something, mother shouts him down like a child. So he keeps to his silence as if that silence were anything to hide in. There are many sores on my heart, Marita. Now that you are dead, the thorns in my heart eat into my whole body so that I no longer feel the pain. Thorns with the medicine of all the pain. It is sunset, Marita, the red of the sky washes me. I walk slowly because of the pain between my legs, but I know I will get there. I will follow the way you walked, a path so full of thorns no one thought you were going to get to the city. But you got there and saw many things before you died. Before they killed you. I do not how they killed you, but you were there with them, searching for the seed of your womb, the blood that you poured out from your own gourd.

Yes, the mother gourd must look for the child-gourd, tracing the footsteps of the child-gourd until the final reunion. No matter how big the eaglet is, it waits for the mother eagle to come back from the sky with a worm in its belly so that the big child-eagle can eat the blood of the mother eagle. That is the way to know the tree of life. Leaves fall to the ground, rot in the soil, the roots drink from the rotten leaves and feed the inside of the tree again so that new leaves can sprout, new buds that cannot stand on their own feet until the seed decays to feed new plants near the old mother plant. That way people are also made. Marita, look for your leaves so that they will not say you did not feed the roots of the plant for the sake of new leaves. Even puppies know it. Puppies, Marita, the little dogs that are born without eyes to see light. Light must not be seen too early, Marita. Light must be seen by steady eyes so that all can see it and remain with calm inside. It is only for the sake of calm inside that the sun must not be seen too early. The weakness of young ones is good. It is good for the young ones. They must not see the sun too early. No, it can kill them because the sun is sometimes harsh. Harsh with eyes that see it too early. Manyepo says so too when the maize starts to grow. It must not see the sun too early. A little sun, yes. But all the sun, no. Those who sit with one side of the body in the sun and the other in the shade know what too much sun can do.

Marita, those who eat the eggs of the hen say the eggs are not good for young mouths. Eggs are good, Marita. Good things are good things. Those who have them always want to make rules so that others cannot get to the good things. If eating eggs is a bad thing it must be so for all mouths, Marita. The hen that has tasted her own eggs never stops to leave some for those who also know that eggs are good. They warm the mouth with new saliva. 'Good things are not for everybody,' Manyepo says. Even when he smears good smells on his body, he says not everybody must have those good things because good things are not for everybody. But why does he not allow even the baas boy to smear those good scents on his own body? Or give the baas boy the way to make the rules? Such a rule made by one who already enjoys good things is a bad rule, Marita. A bad rule for those who did not help to make it.

Mother says I must get married so that cattle can come to her house while she still has good teeth to eat them. But does she not know that when cattle come to her home, I will not have the chance to eat them since I go the other way? What does it help to bring cattle that I do not eat myself? If I cannot eat the cattle that I bring, then it is worthless to bring the cattle to her house. Her husband must learn that the things of one's sweat are the things which one eats well. Not the things of bad rules. My mother does not know the bones I have swallowed. I have swallowed bones which are big enough for anybody with a big throat. So the things inside me are many, so many that all these dark leaves cannot count them. To eat all those bad medicines and remain with life in me is something that makes me strong. It makes me strong because I know the footprints of bad things. Bad things that come from bad chests through bad mouths whose appetite for bad things grows like mushrooms.

Baas boy comes to me and says, 'Little girl, your eyes roam into the hearts of many men, your neck is the neck of a giraffe, your voice is the voice of a turtle-dove, why do you always go away from me before I can say the things that prick me inside?' He growls like an elephant's stomach which has so many things that one does not know which of them causes the growling. I look at him as I walk away, but the following day he does not tire, he comes with much saliva in his mouth as if I were a mango ripe up there in the tree whose height frightens everybody. 'My head bursts with desire for you,' Chisaga says, 'Remember the pots, the pots from the one who made promises . . .' and so the stream flows all the time, leading to I-don't-know-where. Taking with it the blood and the bones of those whose strength has been defeated, the roots and the leaves of those whose strength has been defeated, the grain of the soil of those whose strength cannot endure.

I am here, Marita, walking on the footpath of hot embers and hot ashes. I will get there so that I can spit on my mother's face, that is all. My mother's face has escaped shame for too many

98

times. To let her think that I am the one to erase poverty from the hearth of her house is to let her eat fire. There is nothing wrong in erasing poverty with one's sweat of the hands, as she always says with her own mouth. Sweat of the hands is the thing that kills poverty. Sweat of the hands, nothing else. But to sell me to Chisaga or the herbalist like a goat is to cure her wounds with hot pepper. To cure wounds in the mouth with hot pepper.

There are many things, Marita. Many things in front of me. Now that they have killed you like an ox at the slaughter. Now that they say they do not know how you died but found you already dead. I know that someone does not die unless something kills her. If people do not let it kill someone, then there is nothing to kill someone whose strength is known here even by Manyepo who called you liar when you told him the things that are too hot for his temper. But you simply said . . . if the ears refused to hear, let them go and listen to the buzzing of the bees in the beehive, then they will know that bees sting. That is the way to treat a dog which refuses to listen to its owner, let a stick be used on its head. Then it will know that when its owner speaks, ears must listen . . .

This is night, Marita. Many things can happen in the night. Many things, bad things with names I cannot say in the night, but I walk home so that I can pour shame on my mother's face. My feet cannot see the path they walk on. My eyes cannot see the obstacles which can blind them, but I will get there if I continue walking without looking back. My mind is not here any more. I am not ashamed of it because there is nothing for me here. Nothing, only ashes and broken roofs, and the trees whose firewood I cannot take freely. Only smoke which burns and tickles my eyes, nothing else. Even the water here does not belong to me. It belongs to Manyepo. The air here belongs to Manyepo. Nothing belongs to the farm workers who are so full of fear for Manyepo that if he tells them not to eat for many days, they will stop. Old people the age of Manyepo's father kneel in front of Manyepo. There is nothing the government in the city can do. I rule here,' says Manyepo. 'If your government wants to run this farm, let them bloody take over. Then we will see if they can run a farm,' Manyepo says in his way of speaking badly about things he does not like. Things he despises. People he despises, 'bad smells from these people,' he chuckles when the workers leave his office, sweating for Manyepo to reap from the vast fields which stretch forever.

. . . Sit down and allow the night to pass . . . I hear you say Marita. Sit down and allow the night to pass so that the snakes will not find reason to bury their teeth in you. Rest for a while. Rest. Go up a tree or a boulder. The leaves of the tree will share their secrecy with you for the remainder of the night. Weary muscles lead to a weary mind, young girl. The body is not made to last the whole night awake. Kneel there some time and urge yourself to rest. Pass the water inside you down there so that the land will know that a child is alone on the path which does not end. Do not force the throat to swallow a bone, the elders say. Calm your breath with rest. Calm your mind with the rest of the body. Rest. Even the flowers of the earth rest. They come out today and tomorrow they die out like little fireflies. They leave to go under the soil. That is their way of sleeping, resting for a long night before they come out bright. Rest the weary body. The work I did at Manyepo's farm is enough for you also. I worked so that you do not work as hard as I have done, tearing the skin of your palm, the sole of your feet, the skin of your back, the bones of your shoulders. No, rest. To rest is to allow the milk of your body to come again, the power of your body. If you stagger on, you will weaken the body of your power. Then even the vultures will see you and know that they have a feast waiting for them. It is not good for a young body to be the food of vultures. Remember how they ate the body of Tarega's daughter when she ran away from her old husband. It can happen to you. To fight on is all right, but a good fighter knows when to postpone the fight for another day. A good fighter knows when to stop the fight in order to sharpen the knives for a renewed fight. Young girl, breathe the breath of your rest so that you can meet sunrise with the new fight in your muscles. That is the way to fight. That is the way to walk the path whose destination you do not know . . . yes, I hear you call for the rest of my body, Marita. But you died, they killed you just like that. How can my soul rest? How can my body rest when my soul is not ready to rest? How . . .?

14 **The Spirits Speak**

MARITA will not forget the woman whose body lay near her when people in colourless uniforms went to bury her. She has no memory left, she feels the nibbling of thoughts which pass like the wind, like the smell of a new flower, but where she is, she has knowingness. She has some power, the warmth she shared when she sat with a woman she had not met before. Her thigh so close to the thigh of the other woman, feeling the pulse of the other woman in her own blood. The memory of the woman will always be there, but she wants to complete the work of looking for her son who went to join the fighters. The son who had only started to learn the things of life and death on the farm. The son who always complained about the bad ways of the farm school teacher. The son who knelt only to the girl he thought would be a good mother for his children, a friend to whom he wrote the only letter he ever wrote. No more letters, no more voices, no more breath. Nothing. The sky full of nothing. No stars, no sun, nothing. Also the woman whose husband sold out will remain there in the mortuary for many days to come. Nobody will come to claim the body from the house where they keep corpses so that they do not grow worms.

But the girl still remembers a few of the things Marita says to her all the time. The girl sometimes kneels alone in the darkness of places not many people visit. She kneels and utters, with shivering lips, a few prayers to Marita. Marita, the woman whose breast was dark with many things which did not come to the lips. She kneels to say how Marita made her know many things about the bodies of men and women, young women who grow up to become old one day. The girl says many things until frightening people come to look for her in the forest so that she can remain enclosed in the place where they keep those whose heads are full of bad things, evil things which must be kept away from people with clean heads. She belongs there with the others who talk to themselves without waiting for an answer. Those who remain tied to beds with strong ropes so that they do not use their excessive strength to free themselves. They groan some of the time like beasts, but nobody listens to their story. Even children are there also. Little children who have just come from the breasts of mothers. But their mothers too do not come to see them. They are bad children, they say. Bad children who come to us during hours of evil. Many people are here in the house where people with bad heads are kept. They stare at you all the time without saying anything from the dry lips. No one will hear what those lips can say. Those who keep them treat them like children, speaking in twisted tongues the way children ask for water or food. But it does not matter, they keep them. Marita is no longer with them. She did not come here. The woman who asked for the body of the woman whom nobody knew is not here either, she has nobody to ask for her body from where she asked for Marita's body. They may go to those who know how to try cases and say the chief of the people in uniforms slapped her to death, but her body has already been opened by unkind hands to see what has killed her. It is in the house where they keep bodies. It is there, not smiling. It is there, very cold. Nobody will come to ask for it. No voices will be heard seeking for the body to bury it in the proper way of the ancestors.

The people with uniforms will talk in their small houses where they are kept so that they do not harm others. They will talk everything they want to talk. But they will not say all they should say. They will talk of evil spirits and bad days in their lives, but nobody will mention the spirit of the woman who wanted to bury a woman they did not know. No, it is just a bad day. Things are sometimes like that. Sometimes you meet a bird with broken wings. A bird which nobody wishes were their own bird. Then the sun rises and sets, flowers bloom and die, birds sing and feed their little ones, wives give birth and listen to the voices of the new children crying on their breasts before they name them Tapiwa, Marita, Tatenda, Mudiwa. They will

104

give a name that tells many stories, many paths that have been walked with bare feet.

15 Janifa

TONGUES are bad things, Marita, bad things. They burn the small logs of the heart into big fires which nobody can put out. Big fires, Marita. Think of it, my own mother comes to see me in the house where people with bad heads are kept. With eyes that want to run away from her head, she mumbles like a child who has been discovered stealing milk from the hidden milk pot.

'Are you – er – er – well?' she says with the mouth which has eaten what should not be eaten.

'How can I be well?' I say to her. I do not want her to know all the things which my heart has known. 'How can I be well?' I say, then she takes a thing to remove bits of meat stuck in her teeth. 'How can I be well? This is not a place for people whose heads are well,' I say. 'Do you not see the chains on my legs, it is so that I cannot run away to places where I can sit alone and see the dreams which Marita left me. People here do not see the dreams which Marita left for me. They are good dreams which fall on me like the rains. All the time without seasons, dreams of rains, bones and footsteps falling from the height of a cliff, scattering to the earth while the boys in the field whistle and shout as if they have seen a vulture tearing away the flesh of a carcase. Bones in flower-like flames of skeletons spread all over the place like a battlefield strewn with corpses of the freshly killed whose warm blood flows out of them like smoke from Manyepo's chimney. What mountain have I not climbed, mother?' I say. 'What mountain? What river have I not crossed? What river has not drowned me? What fire has not eaten me? Eating my fingers all the time like those finger-like pieces of meat which Chisaga brought you from Manyepo's kitchen. Mother, every flower has its season. It will bloom when its heart of seasons says you must bloom. I am the flower of this season, mother. Nobody can stop me

107

blooming. Do you know the pregnant woman cannot decide to put it off until another day? Yes, it is like that with me too. I am the axe whose sharpness you cannot touch now. I no longer rise from the same bed with you as I did when the smell of the leaves told me it was time to hear the song of the bird with an ominous voice. I am here in the house where people with bad heads are kept. Here.'

Think of it, mother, tongues are bad things in the mouth of all who use them. Marita said words are little flames that are thrown around carelessly by all those who own them. But here I have no words which can burn because my words are words from a mouth whose owner's head is full of bad things. Nobody thinks the words of the people with bad heads are words with water in them. They are smoke. But to think that a young man comes here and asks to be left alone with me, to tell me that he has been looking for me for many years, many years of searching many paths walked with no success. Many suns sent to rest with no results . . . I looked for you everywhere. I searched even in the mouth of the many caves which swallowed me to hide me from the mouth of many guns which thirsted for my blood. All the time . . . he says, shrugging his shoulders which look uneven like a man who has been carrying heavy things with one shoulder for many years.

'What do you want from me in this house where people with bad heads are kept?' I say to him.

'I am the eagle which had no feathers. I have found where my feathers are so that I can be a true eagle,' he says.

'I have nothing to do with proverbs in this house where people with bad heads are kept. Nothing to do with that because nobody listens,' I say to him.

'It's my mother who tells me where my feathers are,' he says, sweating like Marita from the pain of Manyepo's weeding.

'Your mother? Who is your mother that you talk to me about her as if I have no mother of my own? You are not the only one who suckled from the dusty breast of a woman in the fields. You are not the only one whose eyes swallowed water dripping from the water-pot on a woman's head,' I say to him. But he does not want to stop. He is feverish like Manyepo's ox after a bullet has gone through its head.

'Jennifer, listen to me. You took my place when I left my mother to work alone for Manyepo with his hunger for bigger and bigger harvests every year. You were my mother's only reason for staying on at Manyepo's farm. She died with your name in her heart. But now she is dead, I cannot take my place near her heart any more. I went to fight with guns, but the fight which I have now is bigger than the fight of guns and aeroplanes,' he says, his eyes cutting through the sky like a knife cutting through things that are hard and soft at the same time.

'I do not want to hear the words spilling from your mouth,' I say to him. 'They are useless words which many mouths have uttered before. Go and fight your fights alone without coming to the house of people whose heads are not straight. Go. Nobody binds your legs with chains like these on my legs. Nobody stops you from being alone under a tree to dream your dreams of fights and aeroplanes. Go away and sing the song of the go-away bird to all who can hear you in the village. I do not want to hear the songs of so many birds which Marita told me about. Go away now so that I do not ask the people who keep the people with crooked heads to take you away and lock you up in your own house of people with bad heads, people who do not think straight.' I spit on the hot soil like one whose mouth is full of dust from a long journey.

'Jennifer, my heart cannot rest until you are my wife and I take you away from this house of ghosts. You should not be here, Jennifer. You should be with me in all my troubles, in your troubles.'

I stare at the young man with boots which are hard. They are hard like stone, but I do not think he knows they are hard because he can walk easily as if he has bare feet. Bare feet like Marita's feet as she came out of the fields. Cracked feet which Marita always said were better than shoes because they did not go for repairs all the time. Marita, how you used to work so hard, so hard, sweating all the time so that Manyepo could harvest better all the time. How the skin of your palms cracked all the time and you did not mind . . . I am waiting for my son, that is all. He will come one day so that my sweat does not continue to be watering the fields of the white man . . . Marita would say without much pain in her eyes, calm eyes that saw many things in many hearts.

Marita, your son has come back. He limps when he walks, but he is here. Now that he is here, all the insects can sing their songs and run after the scent of the flowers. All the birds can make their nests and sing from the tops of the trees whose flowers smell with the smell of rains. Do not continue to carry the heart of anger which you carried on your way to be buried by those whose hearts did not know you. Even the woman whose body nobody claims from the house where they keep corpses so that they do not grow worms, she can lie there in the coldness and hear the birds which welcome the child of your womb. Marita, a womb is a dark place, nobody knows what will come out of it. So if it brings out something with flowers on its head, it must be kept under the armpit. It must be kept under the armpit where not many hearts know. Many hearts must not know the things hidden under the armpit, Marita. Did you not say so with the words of your own mouth, a mouth with the sweat of Manyepo's maize fields? Yes, you said so in the pain of the loss of this boy who wants to marry me now. Marita, marrying me is not like plucking mangoes from Manyepo's big field of fruits. It is a hard thing for a man with so many scars from many fights of guns and aeroplanes. To hear people say without shame . . . he married a woman from the house where they keep people with crooked insides of their heads, he had run short of the women who make good wives. Why did he choose to sleep on the heap of manure when his warm bed is waiting for him down there? Maybe his head is also full of scorpions and lizards, many things which soldiers have seen in their fight with guns and aeroplanes. To marry like this is to insult the mother whose womb the young man sat in for many moons. It is a shame that a war can kill such a young man's mind, they will say. They will say bad things about you, things which will kill the nest of my own heart. But to have them say bad things about you is hard for me, Marita, ery hard. It is like the sting of many bees, Marita, a whole swarm of bees stinging us when our hands are tied so that we cannot chase them. Bad. It is bad for the heart inside the chest of a woman like me. It can kill like the thorns that killed the man who wanted to swallow them.

But for now, the sun has risen again from its long visit to the fires which enkindle it. Its fires burn across the valleys of the heart, and the smell of flowers in the heart does not fall on stumps without noses. The sun has risen so that it can shine on the bones scattered over the plains. Even the cry of the woman whose body nobody claims is there in the glow of the young sun so that you can see her smile in her death. She smiles because she knows somebody knows her, somebody can claim her body from the house where they keep corpses so that they do not grow worms. She can stand up without shame and say to the keeper of the place, now if you think nobody will claim my corpse from here for ever, it is only because your eyes have too much mud in them to allow you to see . . . Yes, the woman can wipe away death from her face as if she is washing her face in the morning of her death . . .

And when they have sat down in the shade at the place where they work, they will say many things about this girl who once was in the house where they kept people with heads full of bad things. They will say many more things so that their tongues can go to sleep with tiredness, but they will not forget to point fingers at the place I work and the many songs of fighting with guns and aeroplanes, the many songs I will sing to the ears of those who have died so that the bird which once had broken wings can fly for all to see. A black bird with wings broken by so many ruthless hands that many people think it is not possible for the bird to fly again. Then they will see footsteps of the bones of the woman rising early in the morning to urge all the villagers, all the cattle, the birds, the insects and the hills to rise with the rising bones, to sing with the singing bones . . .

'Mother, is Chisaga still alive?' I ask with hidden fury.
    'Yes,' she says, tearfully.

'Then go and live with him,' I say without hiding my eyes from talking with her eyes. She walks away with her face hidden away from me. She wants to hide her whole body away from me, she crawls away like an injured cockroach, to go to her place of death. She has prepared her place of death already, but I do not want to know it. She crawls away, injured too, never to come back again to the house where they keep people with crooked heads so that they do not harm others. She will not come back because she has gone where the sun has not visited, a place where one does not come back like the sun. I will stand here to watch the rising sun, to see the little animals jumping up and down with the power of the early sun with a new fire to cleanse the infected soil. I will stand here all the time, then walk so that these chains on my legs will have no purpose. Then the keepers of this place will come and say . . . We will remove the chains soon when we know you are well . . . But I will take the broken chains with my own hands and say . . . Do not worry yourselves, I have already removed them by myself. I have been removing them from my heart for many years, now my legs and hands are free because the mountains and the rivers I saw with my own eyes could not fail to remove all the chains of this place . . . Then I will go without waiting for them to say go.

. . . Marita . . . she asked me to read the letter for her again today, every day she comes to me, all pleading.

112